'Exactly what  **to you yesterda his narrowed green.**

Leonie frowned. 'Only that she thought it time the innuendos stopped…' She trailed off as Luke's expression darkened ominously.

'In favour of…?' he rasped harshly.

'The truth, I suppose,' Leonie revealed reluctantly, knowing that had to be the last thing this man would want made public.

His mouth tightened angrily. 'We'll see about that!' he snapped, before striding across the room, turning to look at Leonie even as he wrenched the door open. 'I would advise you not to hold your breath concerning this biography, Leonie,' he grated savagely in parting, the front door closing with a slam seconds later as he let himself out.

Leonie sank down further into her armchair, feeling suddenly exhausted, as if she had just escaped the eye of a hurricane. A hurricane, she didn't doubt, that was now on its way to Rachel Richmond…

Dear Reader,

How wonderful to realise this is my 115th book to be published.

The last twenty-five years of writing for Harlequin Mills and Boon® have been such fun that it seems incredible to look back over that time, to remember with affection all my heroines and heroes. All of them have been so very special to me, so real, that I very often have trouble saying goodbye to them at the end of the book!

Leonie and Luke are such a couple. I wanted their story to go on and on. I sincerely hope that you, the reader, will feel the same way about them.

Happy reading!

Carole Mortimer

KEEPING LUKE'S SECRET

BY
CAROLE MORTIMER

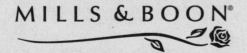

MILLS & BOON®

First published in Great Britain 2002
Harlequin Mills & Boon Limited,
Eton House, 18-24 Paradise Road, Richmond, Surrey TW9 1SR

© Carole Mortimer 2002

ISBN 0 263 83207 4

Set in Times Roman 10½ on 12 pt.
01-0203-45431

Printed and bound in Spain
by Litografía Rosés, S.A., Barcelona

CHAPTER ONE

'DR LEONORA WINSTON, I presume?'

Leonie looked across the room to the now open doorway, having been shown into this sitting-room a couple of minutes ago by the maid who had admitted her to the house, her smile fading to a frown as she found herself being looked at with scathing dislike by the tall, dark-haired man standing there.

'Tall, dark and handsome' instantly came to her mind, although there, Leonie was sorry to say, the compliments stopped. He was also arrogant—from his scornful expression. Cold—pale green eyes were icy with contempt as he looked across at her. And the word pompous also sprang to mind.

But there were also two things wrong, as far as she was concerned, with this man's deliberate misquote.

For one thing, her given name might be Leonora—Leo for her paternal grandfather, Nora for her paternal grandmother—but she was never known by that name, had been called Leonie for as long as she could remember.

Secondly, she was sure, when Stanley had made that original statement to Livingstone, that he had been pleased to see the other man. The man now standing in the doorway of this sunlit sitting-room was definitely not pleased to see Leonie.

In fact, the opposite!

It was there in the scornful tone with which he spoke to her. It was also apparent in the way he looked at her so contemptuously, with those eyes the pale green of a cat, down the long length of his arrogant nose. No, this man was anything but pleased to see her.

And she had no idea what she had done to elicit such enmity in a complete stranger...

She returned his gaze with cool grey eyes. 'Mr Luke Richmond, I presume?' One blonde brow rose as she returned his challenge, unwillingly to allow him to think he had her at any sort of disadvantage; she might not be acquainted with this man but she had recognised him for exactly who he was the moment she'd first looked at him.

Even white teeth snapped together with displeasure, the sculptured mouth tightening, those pale green eyes narrowing with obvious displeasure. 'You may find this situation amusing, Dr Winston—'

'Please call me Leonie,' she interrupted smoothly, her frown returning. 'And I believe you've mistaken my mood, Mr Richmond—I'm more puzzled by this so-called "situation" than I am amused!'

His mouth twisted derisively. 'Because it was my mother you were expecting to see rather than me?' he rasped, nodding dismissively in answer to his own question. 'Don't worry, you will see my mother—eventually; Rachel is notorious for being late,' he added with obvious impatience for that habitual tardiness, moving forward to close the door behind him with studied decisiveness. 'I wanted a chance to talk to you alone before the two of you met.'

Leonie stood in front of the bay window across the room, the sun warming her back—but even so, being shut in the room with this man was like being enveloped in a sudden blast of ice-cold air.

It wasn't just those pale green eyes that made this

man so daunting; he also stood well over six feet tall. His dark hair was styled deliberately short, shoulders wide and muscular in his black shirt, his torso lean, legs long in black denims. In fact, everything about this man—apart from those pale eyes—was darkly saturnine!

Don't be ridiculous, Leonie, she instantly admonished herself; this man might not appear exactly friendly, but his mood might not actually have anything to do with her presence here, he might just be having a bad day. Or maybe this rudeness was just normal for him, and not to be taken personally!

She forced her features to relax into a smile. 'There seems to have been some sort of mistake, Mr Richmond—'

'Any mistake that's been made, I can assure you, Dr Winston, is completely on your side,' Luke Richmond cut in harshly. 'I have no idea what subterfuge you may have used in order to get this appointment with my mother, but let me assure you—'

'Mr Richmond—'

'—it will do you absolutely no good whatsoever—'

'Mr Richmond—'

'—because my mother never gives interviews to journalists—'

'I'm not a journalist!' Leonie cut in with firm indignation.

'—or biographers,' Luke Richmond concluded with obvious satisfaction. 'For obvious reasons,' he added with harsh derision.

One of those 'obvious reasons', Leonie knew, was an unauthorised biography of the screen star, Rachel Richmond, that had appeared in the bookshops two years ago. It had been full of innuendo and speculation about the actress's colourful life, none of it quite libellous, but unpleasant to read, nonetheless.

Another 'obvious reason', Leonie was also well aware, was this man himself...

Thirty-seven years old, obviously handsome, having won several Oscars for various screenplays he had written, Luke Richmond was very successful in his own right. A man, in fact—on the surface, at least!—that anyone would be proud to call their son.

Except that no man ever had...

Star of the screen and theatre for over fifty years, Rachel Richmond had never married, neither had she ever named the man who had fathered the baby son she'd given birth to thirty-seven years ago.

At the time, the mid-sixties, the fact that the actress had been an unmarried mother had threatened to abruptly end Rachel Richmond's acting career, where morality in the screen icons had still been expected, if not demanded, by the multimillion-pound studios.

But Rachel Richmond had remained adamantly single, sweetly silent, instead choosing to take her baby son with her everywhere she'd gone, becoming overnight the epitome of the perfect mother, the whole world seeming to take her, and her baby, to their hearts.

Speculation as to the baby's father had continued intermittently over the years, but in the face of the actress's indomitable silence it had remained exactly that—speculation.

Looking at him now, Leonie wondered how Luke Richmond had coped with the speculation throughout his life concerning his paternity. Or if, in fact, it was speculation to him... Surely his mother, as Luke reached maturity, would have confided his paternity to him, at least?

If she had, he had remained as close-mouthed about it as his mother had always been!

Leonie drew in a determined breath. 'I really think there has been some sort of confusion as to my presence here, Mr Richmond,' she tried again. 'You see—'

'I believe I, at least, have made myself more than clear, Dr Winston,' he cut in coldly. 'I'm sure you're a very capable biographer. In fact, I know you are,' he added with a frown. 'I read your book on Leo Winston,' he explained at her puzzled look.

Leonie blinked in surprise; she wouldn't have thought the subject of her book one that would interest this man. 'It wasn't a hard book to write,' she answered ruefully. 'He's my grandfather,' she explained wryly.

Luke Richmond gave a brief inclination of his head. 'So I believe. But he was also one of the best-kept secrets of the English government during the years of the Second World War.'

'Yes...' Leonie confirmed slowly. He *had* read the book!

'My mother read the book before passing it on to me; she thought your grandfather's story might make a good screenplay,' Luke Richmond drawled as Leonie still looked puzzled by his interest.

Knowing her grandfather, he would be horrified at the mere thought of such a thing!

'My grandfather prefers to be known for his ability as a historian rather than anything else that he may or may not have done in his earlier years,' she hastily assured the screenwriter.

'A genuine twentieth-century Scarlet Pimpernel,' Luke Richmond continued thoughtfully. 'Although, on reflection, I decided the storyline was probably a bit hackneyed,' he added with cool dismissal.

If he was meaning to be deliberately insulting, then he was succeeding. Which was precisely the reason Leonie refused to give him the satisfaction of responding to the insult!

'"On reflection"?' she prompted dryly, glancing distractedly down at her wrist-watch. This man was right about his mother's tardiness; Rachel Richmond was now almost fifteen minutes late for their appointment.

He gave an abrupt inclination of his dark head. 'Your grandfather convinced me it would be in no one's interest—least of all his!—if I were to write his story for the big screen. Besides,' Luke Richmond added with the slightest show of humour in those cold green eyes, 'we couldn't agree on the man who could play the part of your grandfather.'

Leonie frowned at this disclosure; until this moment she'd had no idea this man had ever met her grandfather, let alone progressed any further than that. Her grandfather had certainly never mentioned it...

'I think my grandfather may have been being deliberately obstructive.' She shrugged narrow shoulders ruefully.

The screenwriter looked at her coolly. 'A family trait, perhaps?' he drawled insultingly.

Leonie drew in a sharp breath. She really had no idea what she had done to alienate this man—probably nothing, she reasoned; the man seemed to have a natural antagonism!—but it was certainly time it stopped.

'Mr Richmond—'

'My dear Leonie—I'm so sorry to have kept you waiting!' Rachel Richmond chose that moment to sweep into the room like a breath of fresh air, literally seeming to brighten up the room with her presence.

Rachel also, Leonie acknowledged admiringly, totally belied her seventy-odd years in a figure-hugging green dress, her blonde hair swept back from her beautiful unlined face in a casual shoulder-length style.

'And Luke, too.' The actress moved to kiss her son warmly on the cheek. 'How wonderful!' She turned back to Leonie. 'Why, my dear, you're perfectly lovely,' she exclaimed warmly, reaching out to grasp both Leonie's hands into her own slender ones.

After the son's icy contempt, this woman's obvious pleasure in meeting her took Leonie aback slightly. Although there was no doubting the other woman's warmth was totally genuine; her green eyes sparkled with pleasure, the smile that had been charming theatre- and cinema-goers for over fifty years completely enfolding Leonie in its beaming ray.

Although describing her as 'perfectly lovely' was a slight exaggeration, Leonie felt. In her heeled shoes, she easily towered over the older woman by at least six inches, her appearance completely businesslike in a tailored grey suit and white blouse, her blonde hair kept conveniently short, washed in the shower every morning and simply left to dry in curling wisps. Her looks weren't exactly impressive either: grey eyes, pert nose, curving lips, and a determinedly pointed chin.

In fact, she looked exactly what she was: a historian, like her grandfather.

'Thank you,' Leonie dryly accepted the compliment, very aware of Luke Richmond's contemptuous smile even as she inwardly admitted to being slightly uncomfortable at the effusiveness of the actress's greeting. In fact, she wasn't sure she didn't almost prefer Luke Richmond's coldness. Almost...

'I think you should release Dr Winston's hands now,

Rachel,' Luke Richmond drawled derisively. 'You're obviously embarrassing her,' he added with a mocking lift of those dark brows in Leonie's direction.

She flushed resentfully. 'Not at all,' she told him hardly before turning back to his mother. The woman he appeared to address as Rachel... 'Your son seems to be under the impression that I'm intruding—'

'It isn't just an impression,' he cut in harshly, that brief, mocking humour fading as abruptly as it had appeared. 'It's a fact!'

'Really, Luke.' His mother turned to him in mild rebuke, finally releasing Leonie's hands as she did so. 'Leonie won't understand your sense of humour yet, darling.' She gave him an indulgent smile.

'Sense of humour'! Did this man *have* a sense of humour? Only an indulgent mother, Leonie was sure, could possibly think so.

'I think you're wrong there, Rachel.' Luke Richmond's cold gaze didn't waver from the paleness of Leonie's face as he answered his mother. 'I believe Dr Winston understands me only too well,' he added challengingly.

Oh, she understood him, all right—he was just completely wrong in his obvious conclusions concerning her presence in his mother's home.

She turned back to the older woman. 'Miss Richmond—'

'Please do call me Rachel,' the actress instantly invited, still smiling warmly. 'Luke, darling, did you ask Janet to organise some tea for us all?' She arched blonde brows at her son.

His mouth tightened grimly. 'No—'

'Then do so, darling,' his mother interrupted imperiously before turning back to smile at Leonie once again. 'Leonie, I'm sure you would like a stroll in the garden while we wait for our tea.' Without waiting for an answer she linked her arm with Leonie's and led the way out the French windows into the sunlit garden. 'I do so want you to tell me all about yourself, my dear,' she encouraged interestedly. 'I've never met a female historian before. It must be so exhilarating to excel in such a male-dominated subject. Exactly what…?'

Leonie was only half listening to the older woman as she chattered on, seemingly not really requiring an answer to her questions. At least, Leonie didn't give her any. She was too distracted by the furious expression she had seen on Luke Richmond's face as the two women walked outside into the garden. It was more than obvious to her that if he could have forcibly removed her from the house without upsetting his mother, then he would have done so.

'It really is lovely to meet you, my dear.' Rachel Richmond squeezed her arm in delight, green eyes glowing as she smiled. 'I did so enjoy your last book.'

'My first book,' Leonie corrected dryly. 'But also my last,' she added ruefully. 'You see—'

'Oh, I do so hope not, Leonie—I may call you Leonie, I hope?' Rachel Richmond prompted belatedly, a slight frown marring the actress's otherwise smoothly creamy brow.

'Of course,' she accepted dismissively. 'But, Miss Richmond—'

'And you really must call me Rachel,' the older woman invited again lightly. 'Everybody does. Even Luke,' she added affectionately.

A fact Leonie had already noted—and found strangely odd. And, in truth, she wasn't sure she could use such a familiarity herself. This woman was an icon of the theatre and cinema, still able to command the interest of a crowd whenever she chose to make a public appearance, still able to draw a full audience night after night on the rare occasions she agreed to appear on the stage. As Leonie was finding, her personality was just as commanding in the flesh...

She frowned. 'Rachel,' she conceded awkwardly. 'Your son seemed to think—'

'You really mustn't mind Luke.' The other woman smiled indulgently. 'He's very protective of me. And he's always been such a serious boy,' she added affectionately.

'Boy?' At thirty-seven, Luke Richmond could hardly be called that!

Rachel laughed softly at Leonie's stunned expression. 'He'll always be a boy to me.' She smiled. 'And, I do assure you, his bark is so much worse than his bite,' she excused lightly.

Somehow Leonie seriously doubted that, had every reason to believe he would have forcibly ejected her from the house if his mother hadn't appeared so precipitously.

And late...

'Perhaps,' she conceded disinterestedly.

After all, Luke Richmond's arrogance was completely unimportant to her; he wasn't a man she intended being in the company of any more than she had to. Which amounted to a simple goodbye when she left in a few minutes' time, as far as she was concerned!

Leonie gave another glance at her wrist-watch. 'It's getting rather late, Miss Richmond—Rachel,' she corrected as the older woman gave a little moue of rebuke for her continued formality. 'I—'

'How long did it take you to drive down here?' the actress asked interestedly.

'Just over an hour,' Leonie answered frowningly. 'I'm afraid I do have another appointment in town this evening, so—'

'It was so good of you to give up your Saturday afternoon in order to drive down here.' Rachel nodded. 'I get up to London all too seldom nowadays, I'm afraid,' she confided ruefully.

'Not at all,' Leonie dismissed. 'But I really will have to be going shortly, so—'

'Don't you just love the springtime?' Rachel seemed not to have heard her last comment, looking around the garden with obvious pleasure in the early colourful blooms that already abounded in the numerous flower beds. 'Everything is so new. Life replenished,' she added wistfully.

As it happened, Leonie did like the spring, but more practically because it meant an end to the dark winter evenings and mornings, hating the fact that during the winter months she often arrived at her job at the university in the dark, and also left in the dark.

'Yes,' she answered dismissively. 'Rachel, you telephoned me completely out of the blue last week and asked for this meeting; don't you think it would be helpful if you were to tell me why?' she added with a frown.

In fact, Leonie had been caught completely off guard when summoned to a telephone call at the university eight days ago, only to discover that the caller was the actress Rachel Richmond. She had been so thrown by the identity of the caller that she had agreed to this meeting while still in a daze.

Although it was obvious from the few insulting remarks Luke Richmond had thrown at her that he was under the impression that she had asked for this meeting.

A fact Leonie would have been only too happy to have corrected for him—if he had given her the opportunity. Which he most definitely hadn't!

But despite having had plenty of time for thought since Rachel's call Leonie was no nearer knowing the reason for this meeting. She had even enlisted Jeremy's help, but he had simply teased her about 'hobnobbing with the rich and famous'. Other than that he had been no help in finding a solution either.

Jeremy...

Leonie found herself smiling as she thought of her fellow lecturer, a computer whizkid, who managed to transmit his love for the technology to the students who flocked to join his degree course year after year.

An attraction of opposites, Leonie accepted with a rueful smile. Leonie, with her love and interest firmly fixed in the past, Jeremy, with his lightning-speed acceptance and understanding of an advanced technology that he was sure would dominate the future.

He was also the reason she didn't want to be late back to town, the two of them having a dinner date for this evening...

Rachel unlinked her arm from Leonie's as she turned to look at her, suddenly serious, the green eyes no longer glowing with warmth but darkly searching, looking more like her seventy-odd years now that she was no longer smiling. 'But surely it's obvious why I telephoned you, my dear?' She frowned quizzically.

Leonie gave a rueful grimace, shaking her head in obvious puzzlement. 'Not to me. All you would say on the telephone last week was that you wanted to talk to me,' she reminded lightly.

'But—' Rachel shook her head. 'You mean you have absolutely no idea why I invited you here?' She sounded incredulous.

'None at all,' Leonie confirmed with a good-humoured grimace.

'I see.' Rachel frowned. 'Oh, dear. Well, that makes things rather awkward, doesn't it?' she realised ruefully. 'You see, I read your book on Leo Winston—'

'So—so your son informed me.' Somehow Leonie couldn't bring herself to call that arrogantly cold man by his first name! 'I believe he also read it.' Her voice hardened as she remembered the disparaging comment he had made. 'I'm pleased you liked it, of course, deeply flattered—'

'My dear girl, I didn't ask you all the way down here just to compliment you on your book,' Rachel assured her chidingly. 'I could quite easily have done that on the telephone. No, my dear Leonie, I asked you here because I want you to write *my* biography. An official biography this time,' she added with a certain steeliness in her tone for the previous effort that had so recently appeared.

Leonie stared at the older woman.

She wanted her to—

Rachel couldn't be serious!

CHAPTER TWO

'IS SHE serious?' Jeremy gaped at Leonie across the width of the dinner table later that evening.

'She says she is,' Leonie confirmed slowly. 'That she's been looking for the right person to write the truth for years—'

'And she's decided that you're it,' Jeremy realised excitedly. 'What a coup!'

Leonie nodded less certainly. 'I did try to tell her that I'm not really a biographer...' But her protests had been instantly dismissed, Rachel assuring her that she wanted Leonie, and Leonie alone, to write the biography that the public had been clamouring for for years, that after reading Leonie's biography on Leo Winston she was sure Leonie would write Rachel's own story with the same truth and warmth.

'Of course you are,' Jeremy instantly rebuked, grinning widely, the same height as Leonie if she wore flat heels, as she was this evening. He was boyishly handsome, his straight blond hair slightly overlong so that it fell endearingly over his eyes, those eyes the blue of a summer sky. 'A damned good one too!'

'Thank you, kind sir,' Leonie accepted with a smile.

'But this is—wow.' He shook his head dazedly. 'In view of Rachel Richmond's well-publicised view of biographies, this was something we never even gave a thought when we were mulling over reasons she might want to meet you—I still can't believe it!' His grin widened.

Neither could Leonie. And despite the obvious compliment being paid to her, she wasn't sure she wanted
to do it, either!

It wasn't the work involved that daunted her. In fact,
she was sure she would very much enjoy the research
involved. The reason for Leonie's reluctance to become
involved in such a venture could be summed up in two
words—Luke Richmond!

She hadn't seen Rachel's son again before leaving
the house earlier, Luke not having graced them with
his presence while they'd drunk tea together, but
Leonie had no doubts whatever what his reaction
would be to being informed that Leonie was going to
write his mother's biography; he would believe Leonie
had arranged to see his mother for the sole purpose of
persuading the actress into letting her do it!

In view of that, Leonie had asked Rachel for a week
to think the offer over...

'You accepted, of course?' Jeremy looked at her
searchingly as he seemed to sense her confused
thoughts. 'Leonie, you have to have accepted!' he continued incredulously when she made no answer. 'This
is the story the press have been after for almost forty
years! I take it she will—finally!—be revealing the
identity of the father of her love-child? Of course she
will,' he instantly answered his own question. 'There
would be no point in the biography if she were to leave
out that particular detail.'

Yet another reason for Leonie to hesitate about accepting the actress's offer! For reasons unknown, Luke
Richmond already disliked her enough, without holding her responsible for publicly revealing his paternity.
And she had no doubts that he would!

'I didn't ask her.' Leonie shook her head. 'But I

expect so. It isn't that, Jeremy.' She frowned. 'I just—
it isn't really my thing, now, is it?' she reasoned to
herself as much as to Jeremy. 'You said it yourself last
week—we're talking about the rich and the famous.
I'm a historian—'

'You could be a very rich historian with your name
on this particular book,' Jeremy pointed out determinedly.

A *famous* rich historian. Something she was sure she
didn't want to be.

She enjoyed her life exactly the way it was, lecturing
at the university, going off on historical pilgrimages
during the long weeks of holiday, puttering around in
her small one-bedroomed flat during term time, occa-
sionally going down to Cornwall to visit her parents
on weekends, her grandfather in Devon on others.

Although that hadn't happened too often during the
three months she had been going out with Jeremy, their
Saturday evening dinner together having become a reg-
ular thing, as had a visit to the theatre or cinema one
evening during the week...

'It would seriously cut into my spare time,' she
pointed out heavily. 'Rachel has already suggested that
as I lecture during the week the best thing for me to
do is go down to her house in Hampshire for the weekends while we work on the book. If I work on the
book,' she added decisively.

'Of course you must work on the book,' Jeremy instantly came back. 'You're already calling the woman
Rachel, for goodness' sake!' he teased softly, even as
he reached across the table and took Leonie's hand in
his. 'You aren't worried about us, are you, Leonie?'
He looked at her searchingly.

She couldn't prevent the slight blush that coloured

her cheeks at his use of the word 'us'. Obviously they had only been seeing each other for a few months, and she had no idea how Jeremy felt about her, but she did know that she liked him very much, enjoyed his company immensely. She couldn't see him remaining interested in her if all she had to offer him was one evening of her time during the week.

'Hey, it wouldn't be for ever,' he chided her gently. 'A couple of months at the most, I would have thought. I can put up with that if you can?' he teased softly. 'Or is it something else that's bothering you?' he prompted shrewdly.

For some reason she was loath to mention Rachel's son, the odious Luke Richmond. Probably because her antipathy towards him was almost as strong as his was towards her. And while he might have some idea of his own reason for feeling that way, she had no explanation for the way she felt. Except she didn't feel in the least comfortable with the man...

She hadn't asked Rachel—that would have appeared too rude!—but she had no idea whether Luke Richmond resided at his mother's home on a permanent basis, or whether he had just been visiting for the weekend. But if he did live there, Leonie knew she would find going there every weekend in order to write this book, with the resentful Luke very much in evidence, totally intolerable.

'I'm not sure I want to do this, Jeremy,' she said with feeling. 'I—I have an uneasy feeling about it.' A totally inexplicable, but nevertheless very real, sense of unease. In fact, the feeling was so strong that she had wanted to run out of the house earlier today and never look back. Incredible, but true.

'Is Rachel Richmond still as beautiful as she looks in photographs?' Jeremy prompted interestedly.

Leonie smiled as she remembered Rachel's genuine warmth and beauty. 'Oh, yes,' she answered unhesitantly. 'Perhaps there's something to be said for remaining unmarried,' she added jokingly. 'Rachel certainly doesn't seem to have developed any worry lines over the years!'

Jeremy shook his head ruefully. 'I doubt she's lived completely without male company all these years,' he said dryly.

'No, there's Lu— Her son,' she hastily corrected the familiarity; after all, he wasn't a man who invited it!

'I wasn't exactly referring to that sort of male company,' Jeremy teased, laughing as she grimaced her realisation of what he did mean. 'Anyway, Leonie, you have to admit, it has to be a very tempting offer? One that deserves thinking about?'

Oh, it was tempting, all right, if only because Leonie knew it would be a challenge. As for thinking about it—she had a feeling she was going to do little else until she spoke to Rachel again the following week...

'You look surprised to see me,' Luke Richmond drawled coldly as he stood on her doorstep, totally blocking out the sun that was trying to shine into the doorway of her basement flat.

Of course she was surprised to see him! For one thing, she had no idea how he had found out her home address when all his mother had was her telephone number at the university. For another, she hadn't been expecting him. He hadn't given any indication at his mother's home yesterday that he had any desire ever to set eyes on her again, either!

Besides, she wasn't exactly dressed to receive company, her denims old and faded, the pink tee shirt having shrunk in the wash, added to which her feet were completely bare.

'Well?' he rasped at her lack of response to his statement.

'Well, what, Mr Richmond?' she returned tartly. This was her home, and her time, and she did not appreciate having her Sunday afternoon interrupted by this man in this arrogant way. Although from the little she had learnt of him yesterday, she had a feeling he didn't know how to behave in any other way!

Dark brows rose mockingly over pale green eyes. 'Aren't you going to invite me in? Or is that a problem for you?' he added derisively.

Leonie's frown deepened. 'In what way would it be a problem for me, Mr Richmond?' she returned impatiently.

He shrugged broad shoulders beneath the black jacket and green shirt he wore with black trousers. 'Perhaps it might prove—inconvenient for you, if you already have someone in residence?' His eyes narrowed speculatively.

Deep grey eyes flashed her anger at his obvious derision. 'I live alone, Mr Richmond,' she snapped, pointedly holding the door open wider so that he could walk inside.

'I've never yet known that as a viable reason for not having the occasional—weekend house-guest,' he drawled mockingly, his physical presence making the hallway seem extremely narrow.

And Leonie extremely uncomfortable!

Consequently her reply was sharper than usual.

'Don't judge everyone by your own standards, Mr Richmond,' she snapped.

His only physical response to her obvious sarcasm was a slight rising of his dark brows. 'Can you really see Rachel accepting my taking a procession of women into her home?' he scorned.

Leonie frowned. 'You live in Hampshire with your mother…?' It was a question she had wanted an answer to since yesterday!

He shrugged. 'Most of the time. Like you, I have an apartment in London; I just rarely use it.'

'How nice to have that luxury,' Leonie snapped scathingly; it took most of her wages to keep even this small apartment in London—and she was sure that this man's London home was much more luxurious than this.

'I think so,' Luke drawled. 'Do you have a problem with my living arrangements?' His gaze had narrowed ominously.

'Not in the least,' Leonie dismissed uninterestedly. 'Would you like to come through to the sitting-room?' She pushed open the door to the right of where they stood, leading the way into her sparsely furnished sitting-room.

His mouth twisted derisively as he followed her. 'I thought you would never ask,' he murmured dryly.

Leonie shot him a reproving glance before turning to check that the sitting-room was at least tidy; she usually cleaned the apartment on a Sunday, but she hadn't got as far as this room yet today. Everything looked as neat as usual, only yesterday's newspaper on the coffee-table out of place.

It was a deliberately uncluttered room, completely bare of photographs, the chairs and tables cane, coloured scatter rugs on the highly polished light-coloured wood floor, a couple of Monet prints on the cream walls.

She bent down to pick up the newspaper, tucking it under her arm. 'Can I get you a coffee? Or anything?' she offered awkwardly.

'Coffee will be fine; it's a little early in the day for "anything",' Luke Richmond drawled, looking dubiously at one of the cane chairs. 'Is that thing strong enough to take my weight, do you think?' he murmured ruefully.

'If it isn't, I'm sure buying me a replacement won't be a problem for you,' Leonie snapped rudely, her cheeks flushing deeply red as he looked across at her, brows raised mockingly.

Get a grip, Leonie, she instantly rebuked herself. Okay, so the man was rude and condescending, but that was no reason to lower herself to his level!

'I'll go and make some coffee,' she muttered before hurrying from the room, only breathing easily again once she reached the warm brightness of her cream and yellow kitchen.

What was Luke Richmond *doing* here?

As if she really needed to ask!

Obviously his mother had told him of her decision to offer Leonie the chance to write her biography—and Luke was here to see that Leonie turned down that offer. That alone was enough to make her want to accept it!

Which, in her opinion, was a totally childish reaction. She was twenty-nine years old, with a doctorate in History, was a well-respected university lecturer, and, even if she did say so herself, her biography on her grandfather the previous year had been well received.

But, then, that was the real problem for Luke Richmond, wasn't it?

'Here we are.' She put the laden coffee tray on the table a few minutes later, dismissively registering the fact that he seemed to have risked one of the cane chairs—and that so far the 'thing' hadn't collapsed on him! 'Cream and sugar?' she offered politely once the coffee was poured into the cups.

'Neither, thanks.' Luke Richmond accepted the cup she offered him.

She should have already known that this man would be completely uncompromising, even when it came to how he drank his coffee!

She added a liberal amount of cream and sugar to her own coffee before sitting down in the chair opposite his; she was one of those people lucky enough to be able to eat and drink anything without putting on weight.

'So, Mr Richmond,' she murmured after taking a sip of her own coffee, 'what can I do for you?'

'Well, you can call me Luke, for a start,' he bit out tersely. '"Mr Richmond" makes me sound like Methuselah!'

It also kept him on a formal level—which was exactly where Leonie wanted to keep him!

His gaze was narrowed as he looked round the room. 'This is rather nice,' he finally murmured admiringly. 'Who was your interior designer?'

'Leonora Winston,' she answered with a derisive twist of her lips. 'Interior designer', indeed!—was this man on the same planet as her? As if she could afford an interior designer!

But then, Luke had been born to a mother who was one of the highest-paid actresses in the world, must have lived with her in Hollywood for most of his childhood, and the house Leonie had visited in Hampshire yesterday, although extremely comfortable and beautifully decorated, was more like a mansion than a family home...

Luke looked at her with glacial green eyes. 'It wasn't my intention to be insulting,' he rasped.

'I know that,' Leonie sighed, putting down her empty coffee-cup. 'And no insult was taken. It must be difficult for you to understand—well, just difficult,' she amended awkwardly as she realised she was the one being insulting now.

'I can assure you I haven't always lived with a silver spoon in my mouth,' Luke said.

'No?' Leonie prompted interestedly.

'No,' he confirmed dryly, adding nothing further to the statement.

Deliberately so, Leonie was sure, intriguing her in spite of herself...

'Mr Richmond—'

'I thought we had agreed on Luke—Leonie,' he added pointedly.

She drew in a sharp breath. 'All right—Luke.' She nodded impatiently. 'Did you just come here to comment on my decor and drink coffee, or are you going to tell me the reason why you're here?' she prompted agitatedly.

Luke looked at her consideringly, somehow managing to look relaxed and comfortable despite the fragility of the chair he sat in. Leonie found herself shifting uncomfortably under the full impact of that piercing gaze.

'Does intimidation usually work?' she finally snapped irritably.

'"Intimidation"?' he repeated slowly, seeming to savour the word before giving a shake of his head. 'I'm merely looking at you, Leonie.'

It was the way he was looking at her that was so unnerving—just like a professor she had once worked with who had liked to study antiquities minutely under a microscope!

'You're a very beautiful woman.'

Now he had unnerved her! What did the way she looked—or didn't look—have to do with anything?

'Mr Richmond—'

'Ah-ah—Luke,' he corrected lightly, hard amusement in those pale eyes now.

Leonie stood up impatiently, glaring down at him. 'Would you stop playing games with me and just get to the point?' she bit out angrily.

This sort of word-game might work with impressionable—and no doubt ambitious!—actresses, but it left Leonie cold. She was much more used to being treated with a certain amount of awe by her students, respect from her colleagues, and warm affection from her family; this man gave every impression of a cat playing with a mouse. And she was the mouse!

He was still looking at her consideringly. 'Why do you play down your looks?' he prompted curiously.

She gasped. 'I—'

'Your hair, for instance,' he continued just as if Leonie hadn't spoken. 'It's the most glorious colour, would look wonderful cascading down your back, and yet you choose to cut it so short it's almost boyish.' His gaze was narrowed on her thoughtfully. 'You also have absolutely flawless skin. As for those eyes...!' He shook his head. 'A little make-up to enhance those looks and—'

'When you have quite finished, Mr Richmond!' Leonie cut in indignantly, colour high in those 'flaw-less' cheeks. 'I'm a university lecturer, not some bimbo you—' She broke off as she saw what she already knew to be a tell-tale narrowing of his eyes, breathing in deeply to quell her own anger. 'I prefer to look ex-actly what I am, Luke,' she said more calmly. 'Which is a historian.'

'Like your grandfather.' He nodded, sitting forward. 'What are you trying to prove, Leonie?' The words were launched at her with the speed of a whiplash.

Leonie grew suddenly still, the colour fading from her cheeks, her chin high as she looked at him chal-lengingly. 'I don't know what you mean,' she mur-mured warily. How had he guessed? How?

Luke looked at her wordlessly for several long mo-ments, and then he grinned.

A grin that owed very little to humour, and much more to a rather large feline who had just spotted his prey—Leonie!

'You really mustn't mind me, Leonie.' Luke relaxed back in the chair with a suddenness that made the cane creak. 'My mother, along with most of the fashionable set in Hollywood thirty years ago, sent her child to all sorts of therapists in an effort to ensure that I wouldn't grow up with any sort of—hang-ups about who I was.' His mouth was twisted derisively. 'In the end I became almost as practised as they were in pushing the right buttons to elicit a reaction.' He shrugged.

Leonie couldn't help but feel a certain sympathy for those therapists; she didn't doubt that Luke Richmond had proved a most uncooperative subject! Or that he had deliberately been 'pushing her buttons'.

'Your mother should have saved her money,' she dismissed dryly, inwardly thinking it would have been better spent on teaching this man some manners!

He gave a mocking inclination of his head. 'That's exactly what she finally did.' He smiled humourlessly. 'And you already know the reason I'm here, Leonie.' With a suddenness that totally threw Leonie offguard, he finally answered the question she had asked him five minutes ago.

Which, she was sure, was exactly what he'd meant to do.

She closed her eyes, shaking her head. This man was a nightmare, an absolute, unpredictable nightmare!

'Oh, but you do, Leonie.' He misunderstood the reason for the shake of her head, his voice hardly accusing.

Leonie drew in a deep breath before looking at him, feeling a shiver down her spine as he calmly returned her gaze. But, she suddenly realised hollowly, she had no idea whether that shiver was one of apprehension— or one of total awareness of him as a man!

Don't be ridiculous, Leonie, she instantly admonished herself. This man might be as handsome as the devil himself but that was all he had to recommend him. Luke Richmond was cold, rude and, she didn't doubt, completely ruthless if the situation warranted it.

Did this particular situation warrant it…?

Leonie had no idea!

'I'm sure we're both well aware by now that your mother has approached me with the idea of my writing her—'

'Approached *you*?' Luke cut in forcefully, once

again sitting forward in his chair. 'Don't you have that a little mixed up, Leonie?' he challenged accusingly.

'Actually, no,' she answered with something approaching gentleness; obviously whatever conversation this man had had with his mother since Leonie's visit yesterday, it hadn't included Rachel telling her son that she had been the one to do the approaching! 'I very much doubt you're going to believe me, but—your mother was the one who contacted me, Luke,' she told him huskily.

He stood up abruptly, his face slightly pale as he strode over to the window that looked out on the little handkerchief of garden that was Leonie's. Although Leonie very much doubted that he actually saw the small bushes or the pebbled square that made up that tiny garden...

'What the hell is she playing at? What on earth, after all this time, does she hope to achieve?' he muttered.

To himself, Leonie surmised, deciding that no answer was necessary. After all, she had no idea of Rachel Richmond's motives, either. The truth concerning Rachel's past had remained a secret for so long now, Leonie could see no reason herself why Rachel would suddenly want to change that...

Luke turned back sharply, narrowed eyes that were pale, icy green. 'Exactly what did my mother say to you yesterday?' he demanded coldly.

Leonie frowned. 'Only that she thought it time the innuendos stopped...' She trailed off as Luke's expression darkened ominously.

'In favour of...?' he rasped harshly.

She grimaced. 'The truth, I suppose,' she revealed reluctantly, knowing that had to be the last thing this man wanted made public.

His mouth tightened angrily. 'We'll see about that!' he snapped before striding across the room, turning to look at Leonie even as he wrenched the door open. 'I would advise you not to hold your breath concerning this biography, Leonie!' he rasped savagely in parting, the front door closing with a slam seconds later as he let himself out.

Whew!

Leonie sank down further into her own armchair, feeling suddenly exhausted, as if she had just escaped the eye of a hurricane.

A hurricane, she didn't doubt, that was now on its way to Rachel Richmond...

CHAPTER THREE

'YOU'LL have to excuse Luke, I'm afraid, Leonie,'
Rachel told her ruefully, the two women sitting in the
older woman's comfortable sitting-room six days later
drinking coffee together. 'He can be very protective.'

In this case Leonie wasn't sure whom Luke was being protective of: himself or his mother. But at least
Rachel seemed aware of Luke's visit to Leonie the previous weekend...

'He doesn't appear—keen, on your biography being
written.' Leonie chose her words carefully, only too
aware of how strongly against the idea Luke was. 'I
have to say, after thinking about it,' Leonie continued
evenly, 'that I'm not—'

'I know exactly what you're going to say, Leonie,'
the actress gently interrupted her, placing her hand
warmly on Leonie's arm. 'In the circumstances, I can't
exactly blame you.' She gave a grimace. 'But I can
assure you I do have my reasons for doing what I'm
doing, ' she added huskily.

Leonie couldn't for the life of her imagine what they
were. And she was equally sure that Luke didn't appreciate what they were, either...

'I'm sure you do.' She nodded frowningly. 'But I've
thought over your—suggestion, and I don't feel I could
do you credit.' She smiled. 'I'm sure that someone
else—'

'No one else, Leonie.' There was a steely edge to

Rachel's voice now, those green eyes bright as emeralds. 'I happen to have settled on you.'

Leonie looked questioningly at the other woman. So far in their short acquaintance Rachel had been the height of graciousness, totally warm and extremely friendly. But obviously there was another side to this beautiful woman, a side that could be as forceful as her arrogant son...

Leonie sighed. 'I'm fully aware of the compliment being paid me,' she began firmly.

'Not at all, Leonie,' Rachel assured her smoothly.

'But at the same time I feel it only fair to tell you—' She broke off abruptly as the door was suddenly thrust open, Luke Richmond now standing in the doorway. Really, did the man never just come into a room— knock, even...?

She tensed expectantly, knowing from the furious look on that arrogant face that this situation hadn't yet been settled between mother and son. In the circumstances, she doubted that it ever would be!

Couldn't Rachel see what this suggested biography was doing to her son? Leonie couldn't believe a woman as warm as Rachel could be that insensitive. So why was the other woman being so adamant?

One thing Leonie was all too sure of—she did not want to get caught in the firing line between mother and son!

'Mr Richmond,' she greeted lightly before either of the Richmonds could speak. 'You're just in time to hear me tell your mother—'

'What a nice surprise, Luke,' Rachel cut smoothly across Leonie's reassuring words, standing to reach up and kiss her son warmly on the cheek. 'I thought you were away this weekend.'

'Obviously,' he drawled dryly, shooting Leonie a pointed glare. 'This all looks rather cosy.' He raised dark brows in the direction of the used coffee tray on the table.

'The coffee is still fresh, I'll ring for Janet and ask her to bring in another cup.' His mother smiled, moving towards the bell beside the fireplace.

'Really, Rachel, I'm sure Janet has enough to do.' Luke rasped reprovingly.

Leonie looked at him curiously.

'You're very grouchy today, darling,' his mother teased affectionately. 'I'm sure Janet wouldn't mind in the least.'

'I mind,' he bit out harshly. 'Besides, I don't want any coffee.'

'Darling, why didn't you just say that in the first place?' Rachel sighed, resuming her seat, crossing one silky knee over the other.

The answer to that was all too obvious to Leonie; Luke just wanted to be difficult. In truth, she felt extremely uncomfortable at being a witness to this sharp exchange between son and mother.

She felt even more uncomfortable as she suddenly found herself the focus of those pale green eyes. 'So we meet yet again, Dr Winston,' Luke bit out dryly.

Making it obvious that, if there were any pleasure in this meeting, it certainly wasn't on his side!

Well, she had news for him; it wasn't on hers, either. She had decided through the week as, in fairness to Rachel, she'd weighed up the pros and cons of writing her biography that any pros she might be able to find were far outweighed by Luke Richmond's complete aversion to the project. After all, as the other woman's

son, he would be one of Leonie's main sources of research. A very uncooperative source!

She met his gaze unblinkingly. 'So we do,' she returned evenly. 'In fact, you're just in time to—'

'You really have been very naughty, Luke,' his
mother admonished with light reproval. 'In fact, I do
believe you've succeeded in frightening poor Leonie
off writing my biography.'

'Really?' Luke murmured with amusement, shooting
Leonie a mocking glance before lowering his long
length into one of the armchairs. 'Good,' he added with
satisfaction.

Leonie had stiffened resentfully by this time, glaring
across at the obviously self-satisfied Luke Richmond.
'Frightened her off', indeed! She didn't like Luke
Richmond, or his arrogance, but she most certainly was
not frightened of him!

She turned to smile at Rachel. 'I don't believe I actually said that,' she said dryly.

'As good as,' the other woman dismissed impatiently. 'It really is too bad of you, Luke.' She frowned
across at her son, who looked totally unrepentant at the
accusation. In fact, a cat that had just lapped up the
cream better described his expression of self-
satisfaction!

'No, Rachel, you're wrong,' Leonie put in firmly. 'I
was merely pointing out the drawbacks of such a biography, not refusing to write it,' she told the actress
determinedly. 'In fact, it might be rather fun, at that,'
she added dryly.

'Fun!' Luke echoed harshly, no longer relaxing back
in his chair but sitting forward tensely as he glared
across at Leonie. 'This isn't some damned game!' he
added furiously.

Leonie was well aware of that, but if Rachel was determined to do it anyway... 'Tell me, Rachel—' she turned to the older woman '—if I don't agree to work with you on this, are you going to ask someone else to do it?'

The other woman met her gaze levelly for several long seconds, her gaze searching. 'I do believe I am,' she finally answered slowly.

'That's what I thought.' Leonie nodded before looking across at Luke. 'Which would you prefer, Luke— me, or some other biographer you don't actually know?'

'You already know the answer to that—neither option is acceptable to me!' he ground out harshly.

'But given a choice?' she persisted.

'But I'm not being given a choice, am I?' he snapped, standing up impatiently. 'You can go as far with this as you want to, Mother,' he bit out harshly, 'but I want nothing to do with it!'

Rachel winced. 'There's really no need to shout, Luke,' she admonished gently.

His mouth had thinned into an angry line, fists clenched at his sides. 'I'd like to do more than shout,' he told her unnecessarily, the violence he was repressing easily discernible. 'But you've already made it more than obvious that I would be wasting my time,' he added disgustedly. 'I think I will be away this weekend, after all!' He turned to look at Leonie with glacial eyes. 'I hope you know what you're letting yourself in for!' came his parting shot as he strode forcefully from the room, closing the door behind him with suppressed fury.

'Oh, dear,' Rachel sighed wearily. 'I really do seem to have upset him this time. He never calls me

''Mother'' unless he's really displeased with me,' she confided at Leonie's questioning look.

Was it any wonder Luke felt as he did? Surely Rachel must know what this proposed biography was doing to him, couldn't have been left in any doubts, after this last exchange, how Luke felt about Rachel's involvement in this biography?

A biography Leonie now seemed to have committed herself to writing…

How had that happened? She had come here today for the sole purpose of telling Rachel she couldn't be involved. Had intended politely, but firmly, turning down the other woman's offer. But somehow that didn't seem to be what she had actually done…!

Leonie moistened her lips. 'Rachel,' she began slowly, 'I don't wish to appear rude, but—' She broke off as the older woman began to laugh huskily. 'Did I say something amusing?' She gave a quizzical frown.

'Not really.' The actress sobered slightly, giving a reassuring squeeze of Leonie's arm before moving to press the bell beside the fireplace. 'I'll order us some fresh coffee. In the meantime…' she smiled '…you can ask me whether or not I deliberately engineered that situation just now so that you would find yourself in the position—obviously against your better judgement!—of being committed to writing my biography. That *was* what you were about to ask me, wasn't it, Leonie?' She arched teasing brows.

That was exactly what she had been about to ask! But now she knew she didn't need to bother—it was all too obvious that was exactly what Rachel had done, making Leonie aware that she had better re-evaluate her previous opinion of Rachel.

Oh, she didn't doubt that the other woman was as

warm and friendly as she appeared. There was no doubting her natural beauty, even in her seventies, either. But that guileless expression that Leonie had taken for openness of character wasn't all that it appeared to be; Rachel was more than capable of practising a deception, or manoeuvring a situation, to suit her own ends. In fact, there was more of a likeness between mother and son than she had previously realised!

Although that realisation didn't change the outcome of what she had just done. Because there was no way, without giving Luke Richmond the satisfaction of believing she was indeed frightened of him, that she could back out of this commitment.

The fact that Rachel now looked very like her son had a few minutes ago, like the cat who had lapped up all the cream, did nothing to assuage Leonie's feelings of unease...

'This is a nice surprise, darling,' her grandfather told her warmly as she joined him in his Devonshire garden a short time later, busy in the greenhouse with the seedlings he had grown ready for late-spring planting. 'I have all too little female company since your grandmother died last year,' he added wistfully.

Leonie, despite returning his smile affectionately, felt a little guilty for her own lack of visits during the last few months, aware that it was over five weeks since she had last driven down to see him.

He looked as robust as usual, though, his brushed-back hair a thick iron-grey, his over-six-feet frame still as wiry as ever, the tweed jacket and brown trousers he had on for gardening having previously been what he'd worn during his university lecturing days, a post he had stepped down from over ten years ago to retire to his beloved Devon. Unfortunately, as he had said, her grandmother had died the previous year, leaving him very much on his own...

He frowned vaguely. 'I hope I have something that I can give you for lunch...'

'Cheese melted on toast will do me just fine,' she assured him, tucking her arm into the crook of his as they went out into the garden to sit beneath the apple tree, where Leonie had placed the tray of tea things she had prepared on her way through the house. 'You really should lock the cottage door,' she told her grandfather ruefully as he looked at the laden tray. 'Anyone could just walk in.'

'I wouldn't call you just anyone, my darling,' he teased as he watched her pour the tea. 'Besides, anyone could get in anyway, if they were determined enough, Leonie, locked door or no,' he defended lightly as she shot him a reproving look.

He was right, of course. But that didn't mean she didn't worry about him down here in Devon all on his own. Although she knew he wouldn't thank her for fussing.

A noted historian in his own right, he had continued to lecture until he was well into his sixties, had always been a voice of authority that was listened to, by his students and colleagues alike.

Luke Richmond had asked her what she was trying to prove by becoming a historian like her grandfather. She wasn't trying to prove anything; she just respected and loved her grandfather very much. The fact that she had also known her choice of career would please him immensely had come into it, of course, but it wasn't the whole story...

'So, to what do I owe the honour of this visit?' he prompted once they both had a cup of tea. ' "Just passing" won't pass muster, I'm afraid,' he added dryly.

Obviously not, but by driving to Rachel Richmond's house in Hampshire earlier this morning she had already been almost halfway here; it had seemed only logical to make the rest of the drive to her grandfather's home in Devon. Besides, for the past week she had wanted to ask him about something...

'It's so relaxing here.' She sighed happily, resting back in her garden chair, birds singing in the trees, the wild flowers already in abundance in the well-cared-for cottage garden that was her grandfather's pride and joy.

'It is.' He too looked around them with satisfaction. 'How's your young man?' he prompted interestedly.

Leonie smiled at the description; at thirty-two Jeremy could hardly be called that. Although, probably to her grandfather, in his eightieth year, that did seem young!

'Fine,' she answered dismissively. 'He's away on some computer course or other this weekend,' she added helpfully.

'Ah. At a bit of a loose end, are you?' Her grandfather nodded understandingly, blue eyes twinkling teasingly beneath bushy iron-grey brows.

'Grandfather!' Leonie chided laughingly. 'You make it sound as if I only came to see you because I have nothing better to do this weekend!'

'That's how it should be with old fogies like me,' he assured her seriously. 'Enjoy your life, Leonie, with people your own age. That's the way it should be. Despite what your mother may tell you to the contrary,' he added dryly.

They shared a conspiratorial smile; as an only child, Leonie was expected, by her mother at least, to telephone her parents at least once a week, and to visit them in Cornwall once a month. Thank heavens her grandfather was just pleased to see her, no matter how long it had been since her last visit.

'Actually, I was in Hampshire earlier this morning,' she began slowly, still not quite sure how to broach this subject when her grandfather had never mentioned it himself. 'I believe I met an old acquaintance of yours there…? At least, he seemed convinced the two of you had met.'

'Really?' her grandfather prompted interestedly before taking a sip of his tea.

'Yes. You didn't tell me your social life now involved screenwriters,' she added lightly, grey eyes glowing teasingly.

He gave a perplexed frown. 'I'm not sure…'

'Luke Richmond,' Leonie told him questioningly; she had far from forgotten the fact that the other man had claimed to have spoken to her grandfather concerning his biography.

Her grandfather looked blank for a moment, and then his brow cleared. 'Ah—Luke Richmond!' he repeated knowingly. 'A rather dour young man as I recall…' He nodded. 'How on earth did you come to meet him, darling? Or has your own social life now moved into the world of the movies?' he added teasingly.

'Oh, no, you don't, Grandfather!' Leonie dismissed laughingly—although she couldn't say she disagreed with his summing up of Luke Richmond's nature! 'I know exactly what you're doing,' she assured him wryly, 'and I'm not going to be distracted. Why didn't

you tell any of us that you had been approached with
the suggestion of writing the screenplay of your life?'

He grimaced. 'Can you imagine your mother's reaction to that?' he scorned.

Leonie had no illusions about her mother, knew she
was a complete snob—and she had not been at all
happy the previous year when Leonie's book on her
father-in-law had come into print.

'I can,' she acknowledged dryly. 'But even so...
You could have told me, Grandfather,' she admonished, giving him a playfully reproachful glance.

Her grandfather grinned, suddenly looking quite
boyish. 'What on earth were you doing in Hampshire
this morning with Luke Richmond?'

Leonie looked at him searchingly, trying to gauge
his reaction, but her grandfather was turned slightly
away from her, making this difficult.

'I wasn't exactly with him,' she said slowly. 'I—he
was a guest at the home of the person I was visiting.'

For some reason, after coming all this way to see
her grandfather, Leonie now found herself reluctant to
discuss Rachel Richmond with him. Or the fact that
she had been stupid enough to be tricked into writing
the other woman's memoirs.

Her grandfather nodded. 'He seemed like a very capable young man when I met him.'

'If a little dour,' she reminded dryly.

Her grandfather shrugged. 'Only to be expected, I
suppose. It can't have been much of a life for him,' he
added softly. 'Living in his mother's shadow, I mean,'
he added at Leonie's continued silence, turning to give
her a rueful grimace.

No, it can't have been easy for Luke all these years, Leonie acknowledged heavily. By agreeing to write Rachel's book, she was about to make Luke's lot in life all the harder to bear!

CHAPTER FOUR

'I THOUGHT you were paid to come here and work, not sit dreaming your time away under the apple blossom!'

Leonie didn't need to turn to know the identity of her accuser—if the words weren't condescending enough, the sarcasm of Luke Richmond's voice was all too recognisable!

'Actually, Mr Richmond,' she drawled evenly, slowly turning to look at him as he stood behind the garden chair she sat in under the apple blossom, 'I'm not being paid at all,' she told him dryly. 'And your mother suggested I might like to look through these photograph albums, with a view to the possibility of using some of them in the book, while she took her afternoon rest.' She looked pointedly at the pile of albums on the wooden table in front of her.

Actually, it was a glorious day, the mid-May sunshine dappling through the apple blossom, she had enjoyed lunch with Rachel, and she was feeling rather sleepy herself. Certainly too relaxed and comfortable to feel like engaging in verbal warfare with Luke!

She grinned up at him. 'I must say, you were gorgeous as a baby,' she drawled mockingly.

There was no answering smile in the grimness of Luke's features as he moved to settle himself in the nearest vacant chair to her own. 'And now?' he challenged tauntingly.

Now, if she was absolutely honest, he was more than gorgeous—he was breathtakingly handsome. His hair, in the sunlight, had red tints amongst the darkness, those chiselled features seeming to have a year-round tan, his sheer masculinity also in no doubt in the dark brown tee shirt and black denims. That was if she were to be absolutely honest—which probably wasn't a good idea around a man whose only feelings towards her were wariness and suspicion.

She hadn't seen or heard from him in the three weeks since she'd last been here, but if his attitude now was anything to go by his feelings towards her didn't seem to have changed.

Leonie shrugged dismissively. 'I'm sure you don't need me to tell you what you can already see for yourself in the mirror every morning when you shave.'

His mouth twisted derisively at her obviously evasive answer. 'I thought all babies were gorgeous? To women, at least,' he added with a challenging lift of those dark brows.

'Spoiling for a fight' came to mind!

Relaxed as she was, Leonie was in no mood to give him that satisfaction. 'Perhaps they are,' she replied noncommittally. 'Your mother didn't mention you were coming down this weekend,' she murmured sleepily.

'Didn't she?' he returned unhelpfully, his hooded gaze fixed penetratingly on Leonie's face. 'What do you mean, you aren't getting paid?' He frowned. 'I'm sure you can't be giving up your weekends just for the fun of it!' he added disparagingly.

Leonie shrugged again; it really was too lovely a day for a fight. Even with Luke Richmond. 'I advised your mother that it would be better to wait until the book is written before we talk about remuneration.'

Luke's gaze narrowed. 'Why?'

She gave him a considering look before answering. 'My work may not be what your mother wants. One successful biography, on someone I'm very close to, does not mean I will have the same success writing your mother's story,' she dismissed.

Luke was silent after this statement, as if mulling over the truth of what she had said. Maybe he was; at this moment, Leonie felt too soporific to care what he thought.

'You don't look much like your grandfather, do you?' Luke suddenly bit out abruptly.

Giving Leonie a sharp reminder that it wasn't a good idea to become too relaxed when around this man!

She straightened in her chair, the green tee shirt she wore, with black fitted trousers, a perfect foil for her fair colouring. 'That's probably as well—considering he's an eighty-year-old man, and I'm a woman fifty years younger!' she returned facetiously, no longer feeling quite so sleepy. In fact, she felt under attack!

Luke gave an unappreciative grimace. 'That wasn't what I meant, and you know it,' he rasped.

'Do I?' she returned, her own gaze coolly challenging.

Luke stood up abruptly. 'I'll take you for a walk round the grounds.'

No 'would you like to?', or even a 'shall we?'—just an 'I'll take you'! This man's arrogance could prove extremely irritating if she were exposed to it for too long. Besides, she had little interest in accompanying him on a walk round the grounds. In accompanying him anywhere!

'Janet offered me some home-made lemonade earlier,' she said vaguely.

He nodded abruptly. 'I'll get you some later. Come

on, Leonie,' he taunted mockingly as she still made no effort to move out of her chair. 'I can't believe you find those old photographs that interesting!'

Actually, she had been looking through the albums backwards, from the present day to, as she had said, Luke's babyhood. To her way of thinking she might just be getting to the interesting ones: the time just before Luke's birth.

'It will give you a chance to work up an appetite for dinner,' he added persuasively. 'I presume you've been invited to spend the weekend...?'

'Yes...' she confirmed warily, expecting yet more sarcasm from this man.

She had been shown her guest bedroom earlier by Janet, finding the opulence of the room overwhelming, as she had the perfume of the vases of fresh flowers that stood on the dressing-table and bureau. And that was only the guest bedroom!

Luke nodded. 'Rachel has invited a few friends over for dinner this evening. People who will probably call you ''darling'' all night because they're too damned self-absorbed to remember your name!' he added scornfully.

This man really was a cynic! Although Leonie wasn't sure she wanted to be included in the Richmonds' social scene...

She stood up. 'Perhaps I will come for that walk, after all.' She grimaced. 'Then you can tell me a little more about these guests your mother is expecting!'

'Gladly,' he taunted, setting off at a brisk stride across the smoothness of the huge lawn towards a cluster of trees some distance away.

Leonie had no trouble keeping up with that long stride, having become a fast walker herself after years of hurrying about the university in order to attend, or in later years give, lectures.

'Well, Rachel informed me when I spoke to her on the telephone yesterday—yes, she did know I was to be here this weekend,' he dryly answered the question Leonie hadn't yet asked, mouth twisting ruefully as he saw the tell-tale colour that appeared in her cheeks. 'As you get to know my mother better—which, in the circumstances, you obviously will' he added hardly, 'you will come to realise that her motives aren't always as straightforward as they at first appear.'

Leonie had already witnessed that firsthand—it was the reason she found herself committed to coming here in the first place! It seemed—from what Luke was now saying—that Rachel had deliberately omitted to mention to Leonie that her son would be here again this weekend. Probably because the older woman had already realised that the antagonism between Leonie and Luke worked both ways!

For herself, Leonie was aware of everything about the man as they strode across the well-kept lawn, of dark hair gently lifted by the breeze, those green eyes narrowed in the glare of the sun, of the elusive smell of his aftershave, his movements smooth and sure.

She gave a guilty start, her own stride faltering slightly, as he suddenly turned and looked at her, dark brows lifted in a question.

A question she didn't have an answer to. Except the unacceptable answer that she was aware of his masculinity to the point that her nerve-endings tingled with the knowledge!

Leonie clasped her hands together to stop their shaking, suddenly wishing herself as far away from here as she could possibly be. This reaction to Luke Richmond was not only inexplicable, it was disloyal to her relationship with Jeremy.

Jeremy had been such a dear about her involvement in Rachel's biography, totally supportive, assuring her that they could meet on Monday and Friday evenings until the book was complete.

Her thanks for that appeared to be her attraction to another man! A man she didn't even like!

'What is it?' she snapped when she could stand Luke's unblinking gaze no longer.

He shrugged. 'I was just wondering why a woman like you isn't married. Or are you too dedicated to your life as a historian to bother with such things?' he added derisively.

'Just because I'm not married doesn't mean that I—' She broke off abruptly as she became wincingly aware, from Luke's grin of satisfaction, that she was being deliberately goaded by him. 'What do you mean a woman like me?' she attacked, the only defence, she was quickly learning where this man was concerned.

Luke had slowed his stride down slightly, strolling towards the woody copse now. 'Late twenties, beautiful in a gamine sort of way, highly educated, obviously able to more than hold your own in conversation—and you aren't repulsed by babies,' he dryly mocked her earlier comment about his own pictures as a baby. 'I'm surprised some lucky man didn't snap you up years ago.'

Leonie gave him a scathing glance for his obvious sarcasm. 'Maybe I didn't want to be snapped up,' she drawled dryly.

'Obviously not.' He shrugged.

'Surely the same can be said of you?' Leonie did some challenging of her own.

He looked thoughtful. 'Late twenties? No. Beautiful? I doubt it. Highly educated? So my private-school fees assured my mother. Able to hold my own in conversation? I would hope so. As for babies—'

'That wasn't what I meant and you know it!' Leonie cut in frustratedly. 'I was referring to the fact that you're obviously very much an eligible bachelor,' she added impatiently.

'With a mother anxious to become a grandmother.' He nodded, his expression rueful now. 'A desire that will remain thwarted, I'm afraid,' he added hardly.

'Why?' Leonie frowned.

His gaze had become suddenly glacial, no hint of his previous banter left in the harshness of his closed expression. 'I have my reasons,' he rasped harshly.

Reasons he obviously didn't intend discussing with her! Not that she could altogether blame him; they were strangers to each other, and likely to remain that way.

'You were going to tell me about the dinner guests?' she prompted lightly.

His brow cleared. 'So I was.' He nodded. 'Well, there should be nine of them, four women and five males.'

To give an even number of twelve, Leonie realised. Well, she hoped the man Rachel had chosen as her dining companion didn't prove too socially difficult; Leonie had never particularly liked being forced into evenings with people who were not familiar to her.

'Most of them are in show business, in one form or another, of course,' Luke continued dryly. 'Hopefully you won't find it too boring.'

'I'm sure I won't,' she answered politely, not sure of any such thing.

'After all, I shall be there,' Luke murmured taunt-ingly, dark brows mocking.

Leonie gave him a rueful glance. Was that fact sup-posed to reassure her? No...she realised as she saw the humour glinting in those pale green eyes.

Actually, when he was teasing, as he was now, Luke was more than just 'gorgeous', he was— No!

Stop right there, Leonie, she firmly instructed her-self. She had nothing whatsoever in common with Luke. Except their mutual dislike of each other.

Although perhaps dislike was rather too strong a word to describe how she felt towards Luke...

He made her feel uneasy, instantly on her guard whenever he was anywhere near her. But she was no longer sure that was because she disliked him...

'Here we are,' Luke murmured with satisfaction, coming to an abrupt halt. 'Feel like going across to the island?' He arched questioning brows.

They had walked through the copse of trees at the bottom of the large garden, and now stood beside the lake that those trees edged. It was a large lake, with an island in its centre, more trees growing there. In front of them, tied to a small jetty, was a rowing-boat.

Leonie looked up uncertainly at Luke. 'In that?' She grimaced her reluctance.

Luke grinned, showing strong even white teeth. 'It's perfectly safe, I do assure you. Or do you think I may row you over there and just abandon you?' he added tauntingly.

'It would be one way of getting rid of me,' she con-ceded dryly, even as she allowed him to help her down onto the seat at the front of the rowing-boat, before getting in himself, the boat rocking precariously as it adjusted to his weight. Leonie clutched on to the sides to steady herself as he sat down opposite her. 'Or maybe you just intend drowning me before we reach the lake!' she added pointedly.

'Can you swim?' Luke prompted lightly, pausing in the act of taking up the two oars.

'Thankfully—yes!' she answered ruefully.

Luke nodded. 'Then there would be little point in my attempting to throw you over the side,' he dismissed scathingly.

Leonie tried to look elsewhere as Luke began to row them across the lake, too aware of the strength of the muscle in his back and the bareness of his arms as he moved the oars effortlessly through the water.

'What makes you think I want to get rid of you?'

Leonie stopped trailing her fingers in the coolness of the water as she turned to look at Luke. 'You've never made any secret of the fact that you don't want me here,' she acknowledged with a small smile.

Although if anyone had told her that today she would be sitting in a rowing-boat, with Luke Richmond plying the oars, enjoying the warmth of the day, Leonie wouldn't have believed them!

He shrugged those broad shoulders. 'I think even I draw the line at drowning you,' he reassured her dryly, turning to look at the shore as they approached the island.

Leonie watched as he rowed the boat expertly against the waiting jetty before dropping ropes over the two posts there, one for either end of the boat. 'You've obviously done this before,' she murmured as he helped her onto the jetty.

'Loads of times,' he dismissed distractedly. 'Although not recently,' he admitted. 'It was always my own private place when I was a boy. I always came here if had something I needed to think about. Or just if I wanted some time alone.'

She looked at him sharply, suddenly feeling very much an intruder. But she could see how the rugged isolation of this island would be such a draw for a young boy. Here, amongst the denseness of the trees and foliage, he could be anything he wanted to be; a castaway on an island, a pirate in search of treasure, the imaginings were limitless.

What Leonie didn't understand was, if this was obviously such a special place for Luke, why on earth had he brought her, of all people, to see it…?

Luke took a firm hold of her arm, his mouth twisting mirthlessly as he seemed to read at least some of her thoughts from her expression. 'As you've already explained that you can swim, this would be a good place to hide the body, don't you think?' he taunted dryly.

'Possibly,' she conceded. 'But your mother might wonder what had happened to me when I didn't arrive downstairs in time for dinner this evening!'

'She might,' Luke acknowledged, turning in the direction of a well-worn path. 'This way,' he instructed economically, beginning to lead the way into the thickness of the trees.

He obviously wasn't exaggerating when he said he hadn't been here recently; the further they moved into the trees, the denser the foliage became, completely covering the pathway in several places, so that Luke had to almost fight his way through. But he obviously knew exactly where he was going, the worn pathway always beneath them.

'I'm starting to feel like Stanley again,' Luke remarked, as a particularly stubborn branch swung back and hit him in the face.

'Or Katharine Hepburn and Humphrey Bogart in *The African Queen*,' Leonie came back laughingly as he held the branch back for her to pass.

Luke gave her an appreciative smile. 'So you have had time to enjoy some of the simpler things in life besides studying to be a historian!'

'Of course I have.' Leonie frowned. 'Your mother's all-time classic was when she played the role of Catherine the Great in *Beloved Tsarina*.'

Luke's smile faded as quickly as it had appeared, his expression grim now. 'So it was,' he rasped dismissively, letting go of the branch a little too quickly and catching Leonie in the face with it.

'Ouch!' she complained lightly, reaching up to where the branch had scratched her cheek.

'Sorry!' Luke was instantly remorseful, reaching out to grasp her upper arms. 'Are you okay?' He looked at her searchingly, one of his hands moving to lightly touch her cheek where it had been scratched. 'Damn!' he muttered grimly. 'I'm such an unthinking idiot—'

'Please!' Leonie chided teasingly. 'It's only a scratch; I've had much worse, I can assure you. I was very much a tomboy in my youth,' she said as he looked sceptical. 'I was often climbing trees only to fall out of them!'

'Really?' A strange light had entered those pale green eyes. 'In that case...' He released her to push back the last remaining branches before leading the way into a small clearing.

Not just any clearing, Leonie instantly realised. At its centre stood a large oak tree, obviously hundreds of years old, and about eighteen feet from the ground, with a sturdy wooden ladder leading up to it, was a tree-house. A very sturdy tree-house.

'I always thought I built most of it when I was a boy,' Luke murmured self-derisively as he looked up at the solid structure. 'But looking at it now, I realise it owes most of its enduring qualities to the head gardener of the time!' He placed a foot testingly on the bottom step of the ladder. 'It seems safe enough.' He nodded with satisfaction. 'But I'll go up first and check.'

Leonie looked at Luke disbelievingly. 'You aren't expecting—! You can't seriously believe that I—!'

He grinned unrepentantly, shooting her a challenging glance. 'You're dressed for it.' He looked pointedly at her trousers.

'Yes, but—no.' She gave a firm shake of her head. 'Definitely not.'

Luke stood only inches away from her now, Leonie able to feel the warmth given off by his body. Which was probably just as well; without the warmth of the sun filtering through the thickness of the trees, there was a certain chill in the air.

'Scared?' Luke taunted softly.

She looked up at him sharply, swallowing hard as she found herself mesmerised by those cat-like eyes.

Was she scared? If so, was it the thought of climbing the ladder up to the tree-house that was responsible for that fear? Or was it something else that was causing this sudden trembling and shortness of breath…?

CHAPTER FIVE

'MY DEAR, Leonie—how enchanting you look in red!' Rachel greeted her warmly as Leonie arrived downstairs in the sitting-room shortly before dinner wearing a fitted knee-length red dress.

'Hmm, very charming,' Luke drawled at his mother's side, standing in front of the mahogany liquor cabinet pouring out glasses of champagne for the half a dozen guests who had already arrived and now stood chattering around the room. 'Although somehow I had thought you would be wearing yellow,' he added tauntingly.

Until that moment, even though completely aware of him, Leonie had deliberately not looked at him directly. But now she turned to give him a sharply angry glance. Yellow, indeed! No doubt to signify her cowardice this afternoon when she had opted to row back across the lake and return to the house rather than climbing up into his tree-house with him!

What had he expected? They were aged in their twenties and thirties, for goodness' sake, not children in their teens!

But that wasn't the reason she had turned tail and run, a little voice inside her head mocked.

No, it wasn't, she acknowledged crossly. The thought of being alone with Luke in the confines of the tree-house, when she was already so aware of him, had been the reason for that.

'Yellow?' Rachel repeated in a puzzled voice. 'Why

on earth should Leonie be wearing yellow?' She frowned. 'Not that I'm not sure you wouldn't look lovely in that too, my dear,' she added with a warm smile at Leonie. 'You have the colouring and complexion to be able to wear any colour.'

'Thank you,' she accepted, no longer looking at Luke, let alone acknowledging his sarcasm by giving him an answer. 'Perhaps you could introduce me to everyone?' she encouraged the older woman, having already recognised several well-known faces after giving a cursory glance around the room.

'I can do that, Rachel, while I take round the champagne,' Luke offered lightly as two more guests were shown into the room. 'That is, if Leonie doesn't mind putting up with my company for the next few minutes…?' he added with a challenging rise of dark brows over mocking green eyes.

Her mouth thinned impatiently. 'I'm sure I'll be able to cope!'

'Good,' he bit out with satisfaction. 'You'll need this.' He tauntingly handed her a glass full of bubbling champagne.

No doubt she would—with Luke's sarcasm to contend with for the foreseeable future. Although she intended escaping his company at the earliest opportunity!

Leonie took a grateful sip of the bubbly liquid before turning to accompany him across the room to where a group of four guests stood chatting together.

After ten minutes of introductions, and polite social chit-chat—when most people, as Luke had predicted, ended up calling her 'darling' because they had obviously forgotten her name, Luke having introduced her as simply 'Leonie, a family friend'!—Leonie's head was spinning from meeting so many of the stars of screen and stage. In fact, she felt a headache coming on!

The women were ultra beautiful, their clothes flamboyant, in a wide variety of extraordinary colour combinations. The men were all handsome, and to Leonie's eye with only the differing colours of bow-tie they wore with their dinner suits and white shirts to distinguish them one from the other.

Luke chuckled softly at her side. 'Would you like to go outside for a breath of fresh air?' he suggested dryly. 'The combination of all these perfumes is overpowering. And that's only the men!' he added ruefully.

Did she want to go outside with Luke? To be alone with him in the warmth of the May evening?

Not really. But he was right about the perfume in here; she was starting to feel light-headed. Or maybe that was just the effect of the unaccustomed champagne...?

'Thank you,' she accepted huskily as she followed him through the French doors onto the terrace, drawing in a deep breath of air once they were outside. 'That's better.' She nodded, looking out across the peace of the perfectly tended garden.

'Rachel has no idea how overwhelming her guests can be to the unwary,' Luke remarked dryly at her side.

Leonie gave a rueful smile. 'You make me sound like a country bumpkin!'

'Far from it,' he assured softly. 'In fact, you stand out in that overdressed crowd like a beautiful butterfly amongst—'

'Please!' Leonie cut him off laughingly, turning to smile at him. 'Don't try to make me feel better; they're the butterflies, while I'm the poor drab moth!'

Although there was no doubt that she included Luke as one of those 'butterflies'—he looked breathtakingly handsome in the tailored black evening suit and snowy white shirt, his bow-tie—surprisingly—the exact same colour red as Leonie's dress. Almost as if they had planned it that way…

Which they most certainly hadn't!

'I wasn't trying to make you feel better, merely speaking the truth.' Luke looked down his arrogant nose at her now. 'Do I strike you as a man who comes out with glib compliments just to score points with women?' he added self-derisively.

'As a matter of fact—no!' Leonie conceded lightly. And he had no reason to score points with her, anyway…

'Then accept my words for what they were,' he rasped, turning to face her. 'Which was the truth!'

Leonie swallowed hard, suddenly very aware that she had again put herself in the position of being alone with Luke. As she had learnt to the cost of her peace of mind, only that afternoon, that was not a very good idea…

Luke reached out to lightly clasp her upper arms. 'What is it, Leonie?' he prompted huskily.

Her arms were tingling, she couldn't breathe properly—and it was all due to Luke's close proximity, to the warmth of his hands on the bareness of her arms. Hands that were slowly caressing the warmth of her flesh now…!

'I think we should go back inside now,' she interrupted sharply, deliberately moving away from him, Luke having little choice but to release her as she stepped back.

Whatever was going on here—and Leonie had no

idea what that was!—she wanted no part of it. She was here to do a job, not to provide entertainment for the son of the house!

Luke looked at her with narrowed eyes for several long seconds. 'I'll rejoin you in a few moments,' he finally rasped.

Leonie's cheeks coloured fiery-red at the harsh dismissal in his voice, although at the same time she felt no hesitation in turning sharply on her heel and returning to the crowded, smoke-filled sitting-room.

She looked about her dazedly for several seconds, debating whether to just make her excuses and go to bed rather than try to get through the rest of the evening. She—

'Do come and join us, Leonie,' Rachel invited warmly as she spotted her standing alone, linking her arm through Leonie's to draw her into the chattering circle. 'Leonie is so wonderfully clever, darlings,' she confided brightly to her glittering array of friends. 'She's a historian!'

Leonie almost laughed out loud at the suddenly blank expressions on the faces of the three men and two women who made up Rachel's group. The actress might just as well have announced that Leonie was a road-sweeper for all the interest they so obviously had in her unusual career!

Although she had enough common sense to realise, from Luke's own term of introduction earlier, that Rachel did not want it to become public knowledge that she was in the process of having her biography written. By Leonie, or anyone else.

'Are you helping Rachel with her research?' drawled the rather effete actor standing on Leonie's left.

Leonie realised that the young man was at least trying to show some interest, although, in the circumstances, she could only stare back at him frowningly.

'For her future television role of Elizabeth the first,' the young man enlarged at Leonie's lack of response.

'Oh, I see.' Leonie's brow cleared—although until that moment she'd had no idea that Rachel was to star on television as Elizabeth the first! 'Not exactly,' she answered evasively.

'Oh, well.' The actor shrugged, turning away, obviously having no further interest in her, either.

Charming, Leonie decided ruefully. What a lot of self-interested—boringly so!—load of—

'I did try to warn you,' murmured an all-too-familiar voice close to her right ear. 'Wish you had stayed outside in the garden with me, after all?' Luke added tauntingly as Leonie turned to face him.

'No!' she returned unhesitantly, rewarded with Luke's wolfish grin. 'Do you think we'll be eating soon?' she added waspishly.

Luke eyed her knowingly. 'Need feeding, do you?' he teased. 'Here, have some nuts.' He picked up a glass bowl from one of the coffee-tables.

It took every ounce of self-control she had not to come back with the sarcastic reply she was tempted to make, obediently helping herself to the cashew nuts instead. After all, it wasn't Luke's fault that his mother's guests were such a shallow lot.

'Better?' Luke taunted derisively.

'Not really,' Leonie dismissed before turning to look about them. It was almost eight-thirty now, and neither Rachel nor her guests looked as if they were in any hurry to begin dinner. 'I thought dinner was for eight.' She frowned up at Luke.

He shrugged unconcernedly. 'We're still waiting for one of the guests to arrive. An acquaintance of my mother's who has apparently been unexpectedly delayed.'

'I'm sure that Janet would be only too happy to make up the numbers.' The words were out before Leonie gave herself chance to think what she was saying. Once she had, she realised how bitchy her remark had sounded!

It was really no business of Leonie's that Rachel's personal assistant was only in her early thirties, that she was also a very attractive redhead, that she had shown herself more than capable of holding her own in any conversation with Luke. Or that Luke seemed to like her!

Luke looked at her speculatively for several seconds before slowly shaking his head. 'Not possible, I'm afraid,' he drawled. 'It would upset the balance of the table, you see. My mother's missing guest is a male,' he explained dryly.

What on earth was wrong with her this evening? She had just made a complete fool of herself—and to make matters worse, Luke knew that she had!

'I—' She broke off what she had been about to say as the last guest was shown into the room. A tall, distinguished man who looked to be in his late fifties or early sixties. That current 'male company' of Rachel's that Jeremy had hinted at…?

The older woman's effusive greeting of the man as she kissed him warmly on the cheek before linking her arm possessively with his seemed to say it was a distinct possibility. It was only because Leonie knew Rachel to be in her seventies that she knew this man was Rachel's junior by at least ten years, but with the actress's ageless beauty, that didn't really seem important.

Leonie shot a surreptitious glance at Luke beneath lowered lashes in order to try and gauge his reaction to his mother's obvious warmth towards the older man. After all, it was usually the child's partner who was looked over critically by the parent, not the other way around. Although, in view of the fact that Rachel had never married, this situation couldn't be new to Luke.

He was looking across at the older man, giving nothing of his inner thoughts away in his closed expression, only the narrow assessment of his gaze to show that he had acknowledged his mother's effusiveness at all.

'It looks as if we can finally go in to dinner,' Luke remarked dryly as his mother finally signalled to her guests that it was time go through to the dining-room, taking a light hold of Leonie's arm as they followed the other guests through to the adjoining room.

Leonie had eaten lunch with Rachel in the much smaller family dinning-room. The room they now entered was absolutely beautiful with its tall, ornate ceiling, the round mahogany dining-table set with a dozen glittering dining places, no stark electric light to spoil the romantic ambience but dozens of lit candles flickering on every surface around the room, two magnificent candelabra on the round table itself, a display of lemon and white roses in its centre.

'Wow!' Leonie breathed admiringly. 'Why bother to go out to eat?'

Luke chuckled softly at her side. 'Rachel rarely does; she despises restaurants.'

Leonie found them a little impersonal herself, but as she wasn't one of the world's best cooks...! 'This is

absolutely beautiful,' she murmured huskily, totally bemused by the enchantment of her surroundings.

Although that was dimmed somewhat once she realised she was seated next to Luke for dinner!

Rachel, with the prerogative of hostess, has placed
name-cards at each table setting; Leonie found herself
seated between Luke and the late arrival, Rachel herself
seated on this man's other side.

Leonie had been hoping that she wouldn't find herself seated between two of those self-obsessed pea-
cocks she had been introduced to earlier, but she wasn't
sure she was any happier at finding she had Luke next
to her, either!

'Your chair, madam.' Luke moved to pull her chair
back with a flourish, green eyes glowing with humour
as he seemed to sense her indecision.

'Thank you,' Leonie accepted, knowing she really
had no choice but to sit where Rachel had placed her.
Besides, there was always Rachel's friend to talk with,
too...

'I don't believe we've been introduced, Rachel,'
Luke, once he was seated next to her, seemed to have
similar thoughts as he sat forward to prompt his mother
into the introduction.

Rachel turned to look at him, a slight frown on her
creamy brow as she did so. 'Are you sure that's your
seat, Luke?' she said slowly.

'It is now!' He grinned unrepentantly, picking up his
intricately folded napkin before shaking it out and placing it pointedly across his thighs.

'Yes, but—' Rachel looked perplexed, glancing
around the table. 'I had put you next to Gloria, Luke.'
She turned back to him exasperatedly. 'You know she
and James don't get on.'

'Probably because James finds her as boring as I do,' Luke dismissed uninterestedly. 'Your guest, Rachel,' he reminded pointedly.

What had become more than obvious to Leonie, during this conversation between mother and son, was that for some reason Luke had swapped two of the place-cards. Deliberately placing himself next to her...?

What was she to make of that? Or was she to make anything? After all, it might just be that Luke found her less boring than the maligned Gloria! Whatever the reason, Luke seemed happy with the arrangement. Which was more than could be said for Leonie!

She had been hoping for a respite from Luke's over-powering company during dinner, was finding this whole evening something of an ordeal. Jeremy had teased her last night about going off and enjoying herself for the weekend, and although she was enjoying the research she had so far managed to accomplish, the social side of this wasn't at all restful!

'This is my good friend Michael Harris, Leonie. Luke,' Rachel added in a rather put-out voice. 'Michael, this is Leonie Winston, a family friend. And, as you've probably already guessed, this is my difficult son Luke.'

Leonie shook Michael Harris's hand, leaning back slightly as Luke moved forward to do the same thing, his elbow lightly brushing against her breasts as he did so.

Rachel still looked disgruntled. 'I do wish you wouldn't mess with my carefully planned table arrangements, Luke.' She frowned at him.

'Next time, don't put me next to Gloria,' he returned reasonably.

'He always was impossible!' Rachel confided in Michael Harris after one last exasperated glare at her son.

Leonie had to admit she found Luke just as impossible!

Had his touch just now been an accident, or deliberate? Whatever it was, Leonie found she could hardly breathe after that light brush of his arm against her, and to her embarrassment her breasts were straining against the thin material of her dress, the nipples pert and aroused. Something Luke couldn't be unaware of if he were to turn and look at her.

Which, as if by telepathy, he now did, dark brows rising mockingly as he saw her discomfort. 'Everything okay, Leonie?' he drawled softly.

'Everything is just fine!' she snapped, grabbing up her own napkin as the first course was delivered to them, concentrating for the next few minutes on eating the melon and strawberries in port, deliberately ignoring Luke, although she was also exactly aware of the moment he turned his attention away from her and began a conversation with the woman on his other side.

He was—he was— She had never met anyone as irritating in her life!

Irritating? Maybe. But was that all of what she thought of Luke Richmond? The truth of the matter was, she had never been so aware of a man in her life before! Or so utterly miserable at the realisation...

What of her friendship with Jeremy? The affection and liking she felt towards him? Because she couldn't say, no matter how her traitorous body responded to Luke, that she felt that same affectionate liking for him! She didn't dislike him, it was just that he was like a piece of holly she had once cut herself rather badly on one Christmas: beautiful to look at, but lethally dangerous to the touch!

Not that she intended touching him! It was just that—

'Melon and strawberries not to your liking, Leonie?' Michael Harris enquired lightly at her side.

A natural assumption when she had apparently just been pushing the pieces of fruit around on her plate for the last few minutes. A fact this man had obviously been aware of...

She turned to smile at him, having liked this man's reassuring looks from the beginning; he looked solid and dependable, eyes a warm blue, his dark hair liberally streaked with grey. He was obviously also as much an outsider to this glittering company as she was.

'It's fine,' she dismissed even as she placed her spoon and fork down on the plate. 'I'm just not very hungry.'

He nodded sympathetically. Almost as if he understood the reason for her dilemma...

Which he couldn't possibly, Leonie reassured herself. Besides, Luke was just playing with her. As a means of dispelling an otherwise boring evening, obviously!

'Rachel tells me you're a historian,' Michael continued interestedly. 'With a name like Winston, I couldn't help wondering if you're any relation to Leo Winston...?'

'He's my grandfather,' she confirmed warmly, relieved to have found someone here this evening who even knew what a historian was, let alone be familiar with her grandfather's work, too. 'Do you know him?'

'Of him only, I'm afraid,' Michael admitted ruefully. 'He was at Oxford several years before I was.'

'I see.' She nodded, sure that he was being extremely generous with that term 'several years'! 'What field of study did you go into, Mr Harris?'

'Please call me Michael,' he invited lightly. 'Nothing so interesting as your grandfather, I do assure you,' he excused self-derisively.

'Champagne, Michael?' Rachel offered attentively at his other side. 'Or would you prefer wine?'

'Just a mineral water for me, my dear,' he accepted familiarly. 'I'm afraid I won't be able to stay too long,' he added. 'Unfortunately, I have to drive back into London later this evening.'

Rachel looked disappointed. 'I was hoping you would be able to stay for the weekend.'

'It really isn't possible, Rachel,' Michael Harris told her regretfully. 'Another time, my dear, hmm?' he murmured apologetically, reaching over to lightly clasp Rachel's hand as he did so.

'Why the rush to return to London, Michael?' Luke spoke hardly at Leonie's side, his conversation with the young woman seated to his right obviously over. 'Not too many men would dare to disappoint my mother in this way,' he added dryly.

'I have other commitments later this evening that I simply can't get out of,' Michael Harris answered mildly, looking completely unperturbed by the scorn in the younger man's voice.

'Really,' Luke drawled derisively.

'Really,' the other man echoed lightly. 'Your mother tells me you're a screenwriter, Luke; are you working on anything at the moment?'

It was a question Leonie had been wanting to ask him herself all weekend, but as a means of focusing the conversation onto Luke rather than himself—which was undoubtedly what Michael Harris was attempting to do—it wasn't too successful; Luke simply wasn't like the other people here this evening, was one of those rare people who did not enjoy talking about himself!

But the question did result in the conversation becoming more general, the four of them chatting together about the merits or otherwise of plays and films they had seen recently—Leonie thanking heaven for those weekly visits she had made to both with Jeremy in recent months!

It also meant, with Luke's attention moved away from her, that Leonie was able to enjoy the delicious salmon that was served as their main course, even managing to eat some cheese without becoming the focus of Luke's ascerbic tongue. But she thought she might be pushing her luck to indulge in dessert and coffee, refusing both before making her excuses.

'But it's still early,' Rachel protested chidingly.

'It's been rather a long day for me,' Leonie excused lightly as she stood up. While it may still be early to Rachel, it was after eleven o'clock and, quite simply, Leonie had had enough for one day!

Luke stood up too. 'I'll walk you to your room,' he announced arrogantly.

Leonie looked up at him frowningly. Exactly what did he think his mother, and the other dinner guests, were going to make of him doing that?

More to the point, what did she make of it...?

CHAPTER SIX

'STOP looking so worried, Leonie,' Luke murmured huskily at her side, his hand firmly gripping her elbow. 'Anyone would think I'm about to pounce on you as soon as we're out of the room!'

She could feel the colour warm her cheeks. Warm her cheeks *more*, Leonie corrected; she already felt uncomfortable enough at being the focus of all eyes as she and Luke left the dining-room together. Obviously, as she had already suspected, it was an unusual occurrence for Luke to appear to have brought a woman here. She said appear—because they both knew her being here had absolutely nothing to do with Luke!

But with his mode of introduction earlier—'a family friend'—and his mother's determination not to reveal the real reason Leonie was here, the two of them sitting together at dinner too, what other conclusion could the other guests this evening have come to?

She sighed heavily. 'I didn't for a moment think you were going to do that!'

'Disappointed?' The warmth of his breath touched her ear.

Leonie turned sharply—and then wished she hadn't; he really was standing as close as that warmly caressing breath had implied, his face only inches away from her own now.

'Smile,' he advised tauntingly. 'After all, we are still on show,' he added with obvious derision for the attention that was still being focused their way.

Leonie's smile was more of a grimace. 'There really was no need for you to accompany me,' she said crossly once they were finally out of the room, firmly removing her arm from his grasp as she turned to face him in the hallway. 'What on earth are those people in there going to think?' she added impatiently.

'I'm not sure most of them are capable of thinking of anything, apart from themselves,' Luke drawled dismissively. 'Although they may just think I'm being a caring host,' he suggested pointedly. 'But what does it matter what they think, anyway?' he continued impatiently as Leonie still frowned. 'It's unlikely that you'll ever see any of them again.' He shrugged uninterestedly.

That was true. Although that really wasn't the point...

'Don't tell me, your boyfriend wouldn't like it?' Luke bit out scornfully.

She had no idea what Jeremy would make of this evening. Or indeed, Luke Richmond. She and Jeremy spent enjoyable evenings together a couple of times a week, but there had been no declaration of feelings, on either side. But, even so...

'So there is a boyfriend, after all...' Luke murmured as his pale gaze rested speculatively on her confused expression. 'Another historian?'

'As it happens—no,' Leonie answered him dryly. 'Not that it's any of your business,' she added crossly.

'It isn't?' Luke challenged softly. 'Do you intend telling him about our little walk together earlier today? Of our boat-ride over to the island?'

She swallowed hard, not sure what she was going to tell Jeremy yet.

'Or that I kissed you?' Luke added softly.

Leonie gave him a startled look at this last claim, her cheeks once again fiery-red. 'But you didn't—' She didn't get any further as Luke's mouth came down firmly on her own, his arms moving about the slenderness of her waist as he moulded the soft curves of her body to his harder one.

Well, he hadn't kissed her before—but he most certainly was now! Very thoroughly!

Leonie felt as if she had been swept into the eye of the hurricane that she was quickly learning was Luke Richmond, as if everything else around her were in turmoil, that there were only Luke, and the warm strength of his arms about her, the sensuous pleasure of his lips as they moved against hers.

As her own lips responded!

Her pulse was racing as her arms encircled Luke's neck, her body on fire, her lower limbs fluid. She—

'Really, Luke, could you find somewhere a little more—discreet, if you wish to continue kissing Leonie in this way?'

Leonie had turned to ice at the first sound of Rachel's voice, now she turned sharply within the confines of Luke's arms, finding herself face to face, not just with Rachel, but with Michael Harris as well. Obviously the other man had been about to take his departure—until he'd found his exit blocked by Luke and Leonie…!

'Rachel!' she gasped her dismay. 'I—this isn't—we—' She broke off, groaning her embarrassment. She had wondered about the guests earlier, but now she wondered what on earth Rachel was going to think of her!

When had she become so anxious about other people's opinions? Or had she always been this way? If she had, she hadn't been aware of it. Until this moment...

Luke released her with such abruptness that the removal of the warmth of his body next to hers was like being hit by a blast of icy air. The coldness in his gaze as it raked briefly over her before he looked at his mother made Leonie shiver in reaction, her first impulse to wrap her arms protectively about herself. If she weren't sure that would make Luke view her even more scathingly...

'I do believe you've embarrassed Leonie, Mother,' Luke bit out in harsh challenge.

Rachel returned her son's gaze unflinchingly, her usual warmth replaced by dark disapproval. 'I believe that was your prerogative, Luke,' she rasped back angrily. 'Even knowing—'

'Rachel, perhaps this isn't the time, or the place, for the two of you to discuss this,' Michael Harris cut in placatingly, at the same time shooting Leonie a reassuring smile.

Leonie wished she didn't look as if she needed that reassurance! After all, she was twenty-nine years old, had certainly been kissed before, and neither she nor Luke was married or engaged to anyone else. Under any other circumstances—namely, without Rachel's unexpected appearance, accompanied by her guest— the kiss she and Luke had just shared could easily have been dismissed. If not forgotten...

Rachel made a visible effort to disperse her unaccustomed anger, even managing a smile that bordered on exasperation. 'I really am sorry about this, Leonie.' She reached out and grasped Leonie's icy-cold hands. 'Perhaps I shouldn't have spoilt Luke so much when he was a child—then he wouldn't have the mistaken idea that he can just take what he wants, when he wants it. And ignore the consequences,' she added with another censorious glance in her son's direction.

Somehow Rachel's apology on her son's behalf, her obvious anger with Luke, only succeeded in making Leonie feel worse. After all, she hadn't exactly been repulsing Luke's kisses when the other woman and Michael Harris had left the dining-room so unexpectedly!

The derision in Luke's expression, when Leonie dared a sideways glance in his direction, seemed to imply he was thinking much the same thing!

Leonie straightened defensively. 'Think nothing of it, Rachel,' she dismissed. 'Once again, it was nice meeting you, Michael.' She gave the older man what she hoped was a smile, before turning and making her way down the hallway to the stairs that led up to her bedroom, forcing herself to take them one at a time, determined not to look as if she felt as if the devil himself were at her heels!

But once in her bedroom her courage deserted her, her legs feeling shaky as she made her way across the room to sink down onto the bed, burying her face in her hands.

Had she known from the first moment she saw Luke Richmond that something like this was going to happen? Was this the real reason, that complete awareness she had of Luke, for her uncertainty about coming here and working with Rachel on the biography?

How could she possibly have known?

Because she had known! She had felt the draw of Luke from the first, had known then that she wanted no part of it, or of him, that she liked her life the way it was, and that Luke Richmond, with his lethal brand of sensual charisma, could destroy all that, that he somehow had the power to invoke in her a dissatisfaction with everything in her life she held dear.

For example, she already knew that the lukewarm relationship she had with Jeremy was going nowhere, that if she had been going to fall in love with him then she would have done so by now.

As she already had with Luke…?

No!

Love was putting too fine a word on what she felt towards Luke! Sexual attraction. Fascination. Head-spinning awareness. Yes, all those. But not love. She couldn't possibly love a man who was so determined never to let anyone behind the defences he had built around his own heart…

'I really do apologise for Luke's behaviour last night.' Rachel's irritation with her son was still evident in her voice as she faced Leonie across the breakfast table the next morning. 'He's trying to frighten you off, of course,' she added impatiently. 'I do hope you aren't going to let him do so, my dear?' She looked anxiously.

Leonie had only come downstairs a few minutes ago, deliberately late, in the hopes that she might be able to breakfast alone. Before making her excuses and leaving.

But apparently Rachel had been late to bed last night, unfortunately had only just come down to breakfast herself…

Leonie eyed the other woman frowningly over the top of her coffee-cup. Maybe she had missed something—it was quite possible; lack of sleep made her head feel as if it were full of cotton wool this morning!—but she had no idea what Rachel was talking about.

'I had a talk with Luke last night after you had gone to bed,' Rachel carried on irritably. 'I had thought he had acquiesced too willingly to my decision concerning the biography,' Rachel acknowledged impatiently. 'But I had no idea he would stoop to such lengths—that he would— All I can say is that I'm very sorry, my dear.' She gave Leonie one of her warm smiles. 'That I shall endeavour to make sure such a thing doesn't happen again. Not under my roof, anyway,' she added hardly.

The cotton-wool effect seemed to be clearing slightly as Rachel's meaning became clear. Crystal clear! Rachel had talked to Luke last night, ascertaining he had kissed her deliberately, in an effort to get her to leave, to frighten her off doing his mother's biography...!

Of all the—!

'It would have served him right if I had taken him seriously and turned into a drivelling idiot in front of his eyes, declaring eternal love, and demanding marriage and babies!' she snapped angrily, inwardly so furious that if Luke had been in the room at that moment she might have been tempted to hit him!

Rachel looked nonplussed for several seconds after this outburst, and then she burst out laughing. 'Now that I would have liked to see!' she gurgled girlishly. 'Luke would have been the one doing the running then!'

'Exactly,' Leonie acknowledged with hard satisfaction, not at all pleased it had been so obvious last night that she had been the one doing the running.

All that soul-searching too once she'd reached her bedroom! All that self-condemnation! For nothing! For the simple reason that Luke Richmond was still determined to stop this biography going ahead. By any means available to him…!

'I'm afraid I have to leave in half an hour or so—nothing at all to do with Luke,' Leonie assured her hostess—not exactly honestly!—as Rachel began to frown.

She needed to get away from here today, away from Luke, and the fool he had made of her the previous evening. But she would be back.

'I have a few things of my own I need to do this weekend.' She smiled at the other woman. 'But if it's okay with you I would like to take some of the photograph albums with me and possibly work on them through the week?' At least this way the other woman could feel reassured that Leonie would be back the following weekend!

'It's fine with me.' Rachel nodded with obvious relief that Leonie would be returning. 'I really am sorry this weekend turned out to be such a disaster for you.' She sighed. 'I'll make sure that we have a lot more time together next weekend to get down to some serious work,' she promised warmly.

Leonie hoped that included not inviting a dozen or so guests for dinner; she really didn't want to spend every Saturday evening caught up with Rachel's theatrical friends. Not that there was anything wrong with the people she had met last night, it was just that, as a historian, she was as much of an oddity to them as they were to her. She would never get any research done on this book if every weekend turned out to be as unproductive as this one had!

Although it hadn't been completely unproductive, Leonie acknowledged hardly; she now knew exactly where Luke was coming from with his sudden friend-liness. He wouldn't find her quite so gullible the next time!

If there ever were a next time...

She stood up abruptly, deciding not to bother with croissants, after all; they would probably choke her anyway, the way she felt right now! 'I'll just go up-stairs and collect my things. If you could have those albums ready for me to take with me...?'

'Of course.' Rachel smiled at her warmly.

Leonie made good her escape. Rachel hadn't men-tioned where Luke was this morning, but with any luck he might already have left himself. If not, Leonie cer-tainly didn't intend seeing him again before she left!

It was just her luck that as she turned from putting her overnight bag into the boot of her green MG sports car Luke should come strolling out the front door, car-rying a bag of his own!

'Leaving us already?' he drawled mockingly as he walked across the gravel to join her beside her car, wearing faded blue denims today with a dark blue tee shirt.

Leonie gave him a scathing glare even as her pulse leapt just at the sight of him, a blush darkening her cheeks. 'I do have a life of my own to live, you know,' she bit out caustically.

His eyes narrowed. 'So I believe,' he murmured dryly. 'Rachel seems to be of the opinion that I owe you an apology for last night?' he added in a bored voice.

Leonie swallowed hard, wishing—not for the first time—that Rachel hadn't been a spectator to what had happened between Luke and Leonie the previous eve-ning. That way Leonie could have dealt with the situation in her own way. Namely, by pretending it had never happened!

She gave Luke a perplexed frown as he added nothing to his previous remark. 'Well?' she finally snapped when she could stand the tension no longer.

He raised dark brows. 'Well, what?'

Leonie gave a sigh of impatience. 'Obviously you aren't of the same opinion as your mother!' She glared at him.

Luke shrugged unconcernedly. 'I'm more interested in whether *you* think I owe you an apology for last night,' he drawled. 'Do you?' He frowned darkly.

When he put it as bluntly as that—probably not! After all, she hadn't exactly been fighting him off, had she? After talking to Rachel this morning she did at least know what Luke was up to, could make sure something like last night never happened again.

'No,' she bit out dismissively.

His expression brightened. 'You don't?'

She shook her head. 'As long as we both do everything we can to ensure it doesn't happen again,' she told him hardly.

'Ah.' Luke looked less pleased by this statement. 'I was just about to ask if you would care to have dinner with me in town one evening during the week…?'

He had just been about to—!

'No, thank you,' Leonie bit out forcefully, shaking her head incredulously at the sheer nerve of the man. Have dinner with him, indeed!

Luke frowned. 'No?'

'No!' she said again exasperatedly.

'Something else your boyfriend wouldn't like?' he drawled with obvious sarcasm.

Her mouth tightened. 'Let's leave my personal life out of this, shall we?' she told him tautly.

'I don't see how we can—I'm certainly not interested in pursuing a conversation about your professional one!' Luke told her bluntly. 'Not while it continues to include my mother's biography, at least!' he added.

Leonie gasped at the sheer audacity of the man, the arrogance, the nerve, the— 'Then it appears we have nothing at all to say to each other, doesn't it?' She slammed closed the boot of her car with obvious finality.

'Haven't you forgotten something?' Luke prompted huskily.

'I'm just about to go back inside and say goodbye to Rachel,' she assured him impatiently; as if she would just leave, without making her hostess aware of her departure. Luke might have forgotten what good manners were, but she certainly hadn't!

'My mother's apologies; she asked me to explain to you that she has a headache, which has necessitated her going back to bed,' Luke informed her evenly.

A headache that would no doubt leave Rachel as soon as her objectionable son had returned to London!

Although that was probably being unfair, Leonie conceded contritely. Despite Rachel's obvious exasperation with her son at times, she obviously also adored him, and was also extremely proud of him.

Not that those feelings made Rachel blind to his faults!

Leonie frowned. 'Your mother had some things she was going to give me...'

'They're in here,' Luke drawled derisively, holding up the bag he had carried outside with him.

Hence his reference to her having 'forgotten something'!

'Just throw them into the passenger seat,' she told him irritably before moving round to the driver's side of the car. 'Thank you,' she muttered tightly as he did exactly that, the bag teetering precariously before settling on the seat. 'Please tell your mother that I hope she feels better soon,' Leonie added lamely.

He nodded abruptly. 'I'll do that.'

Leaving Leonie with no other course of action than to get in behind the wheel of her car. Not that she wanted another course of action, she hastily assured herself. The sooner she was away from here, away from Luke, the better she would feel!

Luke leant down beside the open passenger door. 'Drive carefully,' he advised hardly, green eyes almost translucent—and totally unfathomable.

'It's the way I live most of my life, Luke,' she returned tartly.

'Really?' He grimaced. 'The dash of impetuosity in your choice of car seems to indicate otherwise...' He eyed her, and the sporty car, speculatively.

'It was a twenty-first birthday present from my grandfather,' she informed impatiently.

'Hmm,' he mused. 'Meaning you had no part in the choice of model?'

Actually, no... Her grandfather had announced his intention eight years ago of buying a car for her birthday, but the choice of car, and colour, he had left entirely to her, only accompanying her to the garage to buy the car once she had made her choice. But she didn't like Luke's implication that the car she drove was indicative of a more impulsive nature than she cared to admit to...!

'I told you, it was a present from my grandfather,' she returned unhelpfully. 'Now, if you wouldn't mind closing the door, I would like to begin my drive back to London.'

'By all means,' Luke taunted, stepping back from the car. 'I'll see you next weekend, then,' he added mockingly before closing the passenger door.

Not if she had anything to do with it, he wouldn't, Leonie decided firmly as she put the car in gear and drove away from the house down the long driveway to the road. She couldn't exactly ask Rachel to keep her son away from the house while Leonie was there working, but that didn't mean Leonie couldn't ascertain Luke's whereabouts before committing herself to coming down here again herself. Perhaps, with her own upcoming work commitments in town, Rachel could even meet up with her in London during the next few weeks, rather than Leonie having to go to the house.

Coward, mocked a little taunting voice inside her head.

Not at all. This weekend had proved how difficult it was going to be to work at Rachel's home, for a number of reasons. Neutral ground, with no outside distractions, might suit both women better.

Leonie's mood brightened by the second as she approached London, making her wonder if she hadn't just overreacted to the whole weekend. After all, Luke had deliberately set out to put her off working for his mother. It was up to Leonie, by continuing with the biography, to show him he hadn't succeeded.

In fact, by the afternoon, sitting in her own little pocket-handkerchief of garden, going through the photograph albums Rachel had let her bring away with her, she was back to her usual, confident self. Luke

Richmond—pah! If he thought he was going to scare her off with his outrageous behaviour, then he was mistaken. She—

There were several photographs missing from the album she was looking through...

Leonie flicked back to the pages preceding the two she had been looking at. Each had four photographs neatly stuck to the page with adhesive corners. The pages following also had the requisite number of photographs. In fact, apart from these two pages, with two photographs missing on each, the album was complete. And the adhesive corners were still in place, only the photographs had been removed.

Who had removed them?

And why?

More to the point, when had they had been removed? Before Rachel had given the albums to Luke? Or before Luke had later given them to Leonie...?

CHAPTER SEVEN

'SO YOU think perhaps those photographs may have been of Luke Richmond's father?' Jeremy frowned across the table at her the next evening, as the two of them sat drinking coffee together in a coffee bar across from the cinema where they had just been to see a film.

'I'm never going to know one way or the other, am I?' Leonie shrugged ruefully.

'You could always try asking Rachel Richmond,' Jeremy suggested interestedly.

She had already thought of that. But if Rachel was the one who had removed those four photographs, then she had obviously done so for a reason. If the actress wasn't the one who had removed them, that only left Luke, and Leonie had no wish to be the cause of any more strain between mother and son by bringing Rachel's attention to the missing photographs.

'They probably aren't important, anyway,' she dismissed lightly, wishing now that she had never mentioned the missing photographs to Jeremy.

It was just that this evening she was finding being with Jeremy wasn't as comfortable as it had been in the past, that conversation between them seemed slightly stilted. On her part, at least. That, she was all too well aware, was her guilty conscience about what had happened between herself and Luke over the weekend; she knew that Jeremy was his usual cheerful self. She just didn't feel as relaxed with him as she usually did.

Which was a pity, because in the past she had always looked forward to their evenings together.

'Is something else bothering you?' Jeremy prompted gently as he seemed to pick up on some of her troubled thoughts.

Only some of them, thank goodness! It would be too embarrassing if Jeremy were to realise what an idiot she had made of herself with Luke Richmond over the weekend.

'Not at all,' she dismissed lightly. 'It's just that, with these missing photographs as an example, I've realised this biography is going to be even more—complex, than I first suspected it might be.' She sighed. 'It's going to take months of hard work.' Especially if she did as little work on it as she had over this weekend!

Jeremy reached out and lightly covered her hand with his. 'I told you not to worry on our account,' he reassured her brightly. 'You're the sort of woman no man in his right senses would mind waiting for,' he added huskily.

Leonie's eyes widened in dismay at this uncharacteristic display of intimacy by Jeremy, verbally as well as physically. Now he decided to show that he was serious about her, after all!

Maybe it was true that absence did make the heart grow fonder! In the past she had usually been available for whatever outings Jeremy had suggested for the two of them; the fact that she was no longer quite so accessible seemed to have deepened Jeremy's interest.

Wonderful!

Having decided, in view of her confusion of emotions concerning Luke Richmond, that perhaps she ought to start seeing a little less of Jeremy, she was more confused than ever now that Jeremy finally seemed to be declaring himself.

Leonie couldn't quite meet his gaze as she gently but firmly removed her hand from beneath his. Even that intimacy seemed too much when her own emotions were so confused.

If she were in love with Jeremy, as she had half thought herself to be before this weekend, then she wouldn't—couldn't—have responded to Luke's kisses in the way that she had. Could she…?

She had no idea. After years of dedicating herself to her studies, her experience in relationships wasn't that extensive. A couple of friendships with fellow students during her own university days that had gone nowhere, several random dates during the following years, and these dates with Jeremy the last few months, were basically the limit of that experience. None of that had allowed for the force that was Luke Richmond!

'It's getting late, Jeremy,' she told him with forced lightness. 'I'm a working girl, remember?' she added to take some of the sting out of her abrupt end to the evening.

The problem was, she still liked Jeremy enormously. She also knew that Jeremy hadn't changed in the slightest degree, that it was something inside her that had done that.

It was also the thought of their goodnight kisses— possibly more passionate tonight, after Jeremy's show of emotion, than in the past?—that she drew back from. Admit it, Leonie, she admonished herself; she simply couldn't be natural with Jeremy when she was so confused over her feelings towards Luke! In fact, she had met Jeremy this evening with the intention of cooling their friendship, not deepening it…

'Of course,' Jeremy agreed readily enough, standing up to help her put her jacket on.

'Thank you for this evening. I—I enjoyed the film,' Leonie added in a strained voice as they walked outside, grateful for the fact that, because they had both worked late this evening, they had each arrived at the cinema in their own cars. A public parting was sure to be less demonstrative than if Jeremy had driven her home.

Jeremy nodded, seeming unaware now of Leonie's troubled thoughts. 'I'll walk you to your car.'

'There's no need to do that,' she refused with a lightness she was far from feeling, reaching up to kiss him on the cheek before turning to walk the short distance to her parked car.

'Leonie…?' Jeremy called after her.

She turned reluctantly, knowing she was behaving badly, but suddenly anxious to get away. 'Yes?' She frowned.

Jeremy merely looked puzzled by her abrupt departure. 'I'll call you later in the week, shall I?'

'Yes,' she answered with some relief—she had thought he had been going to question her strange behaviour! 'Do that.' She nodded dismissively. 'Have a good week,' she added before getting into her car and driving away with a brief wave of her hand.

Jeremy was still standing where she had left him, looking slightly bemused now.

As well he might, Leonie acknowledged self-disgustedly. She had behaved like a startled schoolgirl all evening, instead of the responsible professional woman she actually was. And it was all Luke Richmond's fault, she thought angrily. The man had been playing with her emotions all weekend—for his own ends, obviously!—but even knowing that did not alter the fact that her own emotions were now in turmoil.

She had valued her friendship with Jeremy, had enjoyed their evenings together, had even thought, in her more retrospective moments, that the relationship might be going somewhere. But that was the problem, she *had* thought all those things. She no longer believed them...

'I do so adore being in town,' Rachel was telling her with enthusiasm.

Leonie looked around them at the luxury of the suite Rachel was staying in for her three-day visit to London, to talk with the director on the television programme on Elizabeth the first that she was shortly to start filming, sure that Rachel couldn't help but enjoy staying in London in her present surroundings.

The sitting-room of the suite of rooms alone was as big as Leonie's whole apartment put together, the furniture antique, the fabrics all gold brocades, and there were vases of fresh flowers on every surface available. No doubt room service was pretty spectacular too, Leonie thought wistfully.

Rachel had telephoned Leonie as soon as she'd arrived in town yesterday, Thursday, the actress explaining that as she was due to meet the television director on Friday she had decided to stay the whole weekend, and suggested that the two of them meet up at her hotel Friday evening.

Leonie had welcomed the suggestion with open arms, hardly able to believe her good luck; with Rachel up in town it meant that Leonie didn't have to risk seeing Luke at the family home, and as it was Friday,

Leonie also had a legitimate excuse for not seeing Jeremy this evening, too.

She still had no idea what she was going to do about Jeremy, but this meeting with Rachel had certainly given her a respite from making any definite decision. Cowardly, perhaps, but she wasn't a person who came to snap decisions or, indeed, acted upon them.

At least, not normally… It didn't take great sense on her part to know she would be better staying as far away from Luke as it was possible for her to do so!

'I've brought all my diaries with me from when I first went off to Hollywood aged eighteen,' Rachel told her now, opening the leather briefcase that lay on the coffee-table in front of her, to reveal dozens of small red leather-bound books. Obviously, the diaries. 'They make pretty interesting reading after all this time. Even to me!' Green eyes sparkled mischievously.

Leonie returned the smile. 'I'm sure they do. Are you willing for me to read them, or would you prefer—?'

'Of course you must read them,' the older woman cut in dismissively. 'They will give you an insight into my life then much better than I could ever recall by just sitting here talking about it.'

'I hope you'll remember to censor them before handing them over to Leonie,' drawled an all-too-familiarly mocking voice.

Leonie turned sharply in the direction of that voice, already knowing she would see Luke standing there, but finding the impulse to look irresistible.

He had obviously just let himself into the hotel suite, was wearing a black dinner suit and snowy white shirt, his dark hair still damp from the shower he must have recently taken.

There was no escaping the fact—despite the warnings Leonie had given herself all week that Luke had just been playing with her last weekend—that he looked devastatingly handsome. So much so that Leonie's heart seemed to do a somersault in her chest.

She turned away hastily as she suddenly realised Luke was looking straight back at her with those mocking green eyes, her cheeks becoming fiery-red at the knowledge that she could have given herself away so easily the moment she was in his company.

She should have guessed this would happen, of course, should have known she wasn't going to escape seeing Luke again that easily; because wherever Rachel happened to be, her son was never far away. Correction—wherever Rachel happened to be with Leonie, this man was sure never to be far away!

Leonie frowned at that realisation. What was Luke so afraid of? Did he think that his mother, after all this time of silence, would just throw all caution to the wind and confide in Leonie, her biographer, who Luke's father was? He couldn't have much trust in his mother if he really believed Rachel could betray him in that way. Without even having discussed it with him first.

Unless Rachel had already done exactly that…?

No, Leonie couldn't believe Rachel would do that when she must know how much it would be hurting Luke for her to do so. But Luke's constant presence, whenever the two women got together like this, must surely mean that Luke didn't have the same confidence in his own mother…?

But the way he was dressed, obviously on his way out for the evening—with a woman? Leonie couldn't help wondering frowningly—seemed to imply that he wouldn't be staying very long this time, that he had simply called in on the way to another engagement.

The fact that Luke had just arrived must mean he was staying at the apartment he had told Leonie he had in London. Which begged the question why, when Luke had an apartment here, his mother wasn't staying there with him. Not that Leonie would have wanted to visit Rachel there, but it was still curious that Rachel didn't stay with her son when she came up to town. Although, perhaps not... After all, Luke had to 'entertain' somewhere after his claim that his mother wouldn't appreciate him taking women to her home!

Rachel smiled warmly at Luke now as he crossed the room to bend down and kiss her lightly on the cheek. 'Luke has come to take us both to dinner, Leonie,' Rachel turned to inform her lightly—totally blowing Leonie's earlier supposition, that of Luke being on his way out on a date, out of the water! 'On the condition that he behaves himself, of course,' his mother added dryly.

Luke had straightened now, his gaze challenging as he turned to look across at Leonie. 'Before I make such an undertaking, perhaps we should ask Leonie if she wants me to behave...?' he drawled mockingly.

'Of course I—' She broke off in the middle of her outraged outburst, glaring at Luke as he openly grinned now at the embarrassment he had just deliberately caused her. 'Your behaviour, good, bad, or indifferent, is of no interest to me,' Leonie told him stiffly.

He raised dark brows. 'No?'

'Why do you keep upsetting the girl, Luke?' his mother admonished impatiently as she stood up to briefly touch Leonie's arm in apology for her son's behaviour, looking ethereally beautiful in a simple black sequinned dress, its knee-length revealing slender silk-covered legs.

Luke shrugged unrepentantly. 'It's just so easy to do,' he murmured dryly.

'Well, it isn't kind, Luke,' his mother admonished firmly.

'I'm really not dressed to go to dinner,' Leonie told the other woman, totally ignoring Luke now.

'You look lovely,' Rachel assured her dismissively. 'Anything in black is always elegant, my dear.' She looked admiringly at Leonie's own simply cut black dress, her short blonde hair in its usual windswept style.

Leonie had only put on high-heeled black sandals and a dress at all in deference to the exclusivity of the hotel Rachel was staying in; it certainly wasn't one of her best outfits, and she in no way felt suitably dressed to have dinner with this elegant couple.

She shook her head. 'I really don't—'

'I have a silk scarf in my bedroom that will look absolutely perfect with that dress,' Rachel assured her warmly. 'I'll just go and get it.' She turned on her heel and hurried out of the room.

Leaving Leonie conscious of the fact that she and Luke were now very much alone. If he dared to say just one sarcastic word, she would—

'Have you had an enjoyable week?'

She looked up sharply at Luke's husky comment, searching the hard planes of his face for any sign of sarcasm. To her surprise, she found none, his expression totally unfathomable as he looked across at her.

'Yes—fine. Thank you,' she answered stiltedly, totally unsure of him.

She also wished she had stood up before Rachel had

left the room, feeling at a distinct disadvantage sitting in the armchair looking up at Luke's considerable height.

'I haven't,' he rasped abruptly.

Grey eyes widened in surprise at the starkness of his statement. 'I—' What was she supposed to say to that? I'm sorry? Why haven't you? She simply didn't know.

He drew in a harsh breath. 'Leonie—' He came to an abrupt halt, sighing as he now glared at her frustratedly.

Leonie frowned her puzzlement with his strange behaviour. What on earth was wrong with him? 'I'm sorry,' she murmured questioningly.

'Are you?' he scorned, hands now clenched into fists at his sides. 'Somehow I doubt that.' He shook his head disgustedly. 'I have the distinct feeling you would like nothing better than to see me writhing in the fires of hell!'

Leonie gasped at the fierceness of his statement, shaking her head dazedly. 'I don't think you understand me at all, Luke—'

'I don't think you want me to—dear Leonie,' he cut in scathingly, even the façade of politeness having dropped from him now.

She moistened suddenly dry lips, totally thrown by the fierceness of this conversation after Rachel's warm company. The contrast between mother and son was certainly difficult to come to terms with. Even had Leonie wanted to…!

She drew in a deep breath. 'I'm really sorry you haven't had a good week, Luke. There, is that better?' she challenged sarcastically.

'No, it isn't!' Luke rasped. 'Leonie—'

'Your mother seems to be a long time finding that

scarf.' She looked frowningly towards the bedroom Rachel had disappeared into—was it really only minutes ago?

Luke gave a humourless smile, his eyes that pale icy green. 'She's probably giving me time to proffer that apology I omitted to give you last weekend!'

Leonie raised blonde brows. 'Then she's obviously wasting her time!'

He gave what appeared to be an unwilling smile. 'No one could ever accuse you of excessive politeness yourself!' he murmured appreciatively.

She shrugged. 'That depends on who I'm talking to.'

Luke's smile widened, his gaze becoming less icy too. 'You really are the most— Where have you been all my life, Leonie Winston?' He shook his head self-derisively.

'Avoiding you, probably,' she told him honestly, knowing that if she had met this arrogant man during her student years he would have frightened the life out of her. It was only her maturity, her confidence in her own abilities, that allowed her to meet him on equal ground now. Well…almost equal—he still had the ability to make her feel uncomfortably gauche at times!

He laughed out loud this time, suddenly looking years younger, laughter lines crinkling beside his eyes and mouth. A totally sensual mouth, Leonie acknowledged as she watched him with fascination. He should laugh more often. Or…maybe not. Luke was altogether too disturbing in this relaxed mood.

'Leonie—'

'Here we are.' Rachel appeared from the bedroom carrying the promised scarf of pale grey silk. 'Everything okay out here?' she prompted lightly even as she pulled Leonie to her feet and began arranging the delicate scarf lightly about her throat.

Luke had been right—Rachel obviously had hoped the two of them would make their peace in her absence.

Had they done that? Not that Leonie could recall. Although Luke, at least, seemed more relaxed...

'Friends again?' Rachel said brightly as she straightened, her ministrations to the scarf complete.

Leonie wasn't sure she and Luke had ever reached that stage, let alone regained it!

She looked uncertainly at Luke, could see by his slightly sceptical expression that he had been thinking the same thing. Besides, she wasn't sure she wanted him as a 'friend'...

'I have no idea,' Luke bit out abruptly. 'Are we friends, Leonie?' He raised dark brows.

Her tongue seemed to be stuck to the roof of her mouth. Could she and Luke ever be friends? Somehow she doubted it—they were far too aware of each other to ever reach such a situation of amicability...

Luke's mouth twisted wryly. 'I think the jury is still out on that one, Rachel,' he said derisively.

Rachel pouted her disappointment. 'I did so hope the two of you were going to get along.'

'I'm well aware of what you hoped, Mother,' Luke answered tautly. 'But it isn't going to happen!' he bit out harshly. 'It never was. Despite your machinations,' he added darkly.

Leonie looked frowningly from mother to son, having no idea what on earth the two of them were talking about. But she also knew, from their stubbornly set faces as the two glared at each other—so alike in their obstinacy—that neither of them were going to enlighten her, either!

In those circumstances, this promised to be a less than relaxing evening!

CHAPTER EIGHT

'I ABSOLUTELY adore this hotel,' Rachel confided in Leonie once they were seated in the restaurant. 'It's one of the few places where I choose not to eat in my hotel suite. For obvious reasons.'

Leonie was absolutely enchanted with the restaurant on the top floor of the hotel, too. Not only was it intimately arranged, the staff polite but not overly effusive, despite their obvious recognition of their celebrated guest, but the table the three of them sat at by the window had a magnificent view of the illuminated skyline of London.

Even having Luke seated beside her at the table couldn't dull Leonie's pleasure in her surroundings!

'It's wonderful,' she agreed huskily.

'I'm so pleased you like it.' Rachel, sitting on Leonie's other side, squeezed her arm warmly. 'Of course, having a handsome man to escort us does rather add to the evening's enjoyment,' she added with a mischievous smile in her son's direction.

'I'm so glad I can be of use,' Luke returned dryly, nodding dismissively to the waiter once he had poured their three glasses of pink champagne.

'I always drink champagne,' Rachel confided brightly as she sipped the bubbly liquid. 'It invariably goes with any choice of food, and it doesn't give you a hangover the next day,' she added with satisfaction.

Ordinarily, Leonie knew, this being a Friday evening, she and Jeremy would probably have gone to a pizza or steak restaurant, and indulged in a bottle of not-too-expensive red wine. The way that Rachel liked to live—and consequently Luke, too—was the stuff films were made of.

But, Leonie decided after a couple of sips of the delicious champagne, it was a very nice way to spend an evening. And the food, when their first course arrived, was absolutely exquisite, in presentation as well as taste.

Whoa, Leonie, she instructed herself ruefully. Enjoyable though this might be, it wasn't real life, certainly not her real life. And already Rachel was discussing the possibility of Leonie joining her here for lunch tomorrow!

'I'm afraid that won't be possible,' she told the older woman apologetically. 'I'm going to Devon for the rest of the weekend.'

'With the boyfriend?' Luke put in mildly.

But it was a deceptive mildness, Leonie noted as she turned to him frowningly, his eyes the palest of green, a sign Leonie had noticed in the past that indicated he was far from pleased. As if she cared whether Luke were pleased about her weekend arrangements or not!

'No,' Leonie answered abruptly, knowing that if the two of them had been alone she would have been much less polite. 'It's my parents' wedding anniversary tomorrow, and my grandfather has arranged a small surprise party to celebrate.'

'How wonderful!' Rachel was the one to answer enthusiastically. 'Have they been married long?'

'Twenty-nine years,' Leonie supplied, very aware of Luke listening intently to the conversation.

'In that case, I should think they deserve a medal, not a surprise party!' he rasped dryly.

'Don't be such a cynic, Luke,' Rachel admonished impatiently before turning back to Leonie. 'Do you see a lot of your family?' she asked interestedly.

She grimaced. 'Not as much as I should, I'm afraid. My grandfather is wonderful, but—I'm hesitant to make the universal cry of ''my parents don't understand me''—!' She felt, and looked, rather embarrassed; she was sure Rachel and Luke weren't in the least interested in her relationship with the rest of her family, that Rachel's initial enquiry had merely been a politeness.

'Even if it's true?' Rachel said shrewdly. 'Luke and I have always had the closest of relationships—yes, we have, you irritating boy,' she reproved lightly as Luke gave a disbelieving snort.

'I don't think you were of the same opinion the time I took a couple of years out from our relationship,' he reminded dryly.

'You were twenty-five, and rebelling against—well, against everything really,' Rachel acknowledged indulgently. 'Besides, it did you the world of good to stand on your own two feet for a while. He did the equivalent of ''starving in a garret'' for two years, just to prove he could do it,' she confided in Leonie.

Obviously this was the time that Luke had claimed he hadn't lived with that 'silver spoon' in his life. Although taking 'a couple of years out' of their relationship must have been very hard on Rachel...

'And could he?' Leonie couldn't resist asking.

'Of course,' Rachel answered ruefully. 'He wrote a successful screenplay, and scooped an Oscar, before deciding that being my son wasn't so bad, after all.'

'There was never anything wrong with being your son—' Luke began harshly.

'Darling,' Rachel cut in firmly, 'we really shouldn't air our dirty laundry in front of Leonie in this way.'

'Why the hell not?' he rasped. 'After all—'

'This smoked salmon is absolutely gorgeous; how are your prawns?' Rachel prompted Leonie brightly.

'The same,' she answered a little dazedly, totally thrown by how intense the conversation had suddenly become between mother and son.

'I was about to say, Rachel,' Luke continued determinedly, 'that as Leonie is writing your biography, it may be as well if she knows your life hasn't always been one of champagne and roses. And, if anyone is interested, my escargot are excellent!' he added with obvious impatience.

Leonie found herself slightly resenting the fact that he might have thought she had assumed any such thing; after all, although Rachel made light of it, it really couldn't have been all that easy for her to continue smiling through single-parenthood all those years.

But that resentment faded as Rachel caught her eye, repressed laughter twinkling in merry green eyes. At Luke's expense, Leonie realised; he really had sounded like a rather truculent little boy who didn't like being left out of the conversation!

Rachel was the first to laugh, quickly followed by Leonie, and then—surprise, surprise—Luke began to chuckle throatily too.

'Okay, okay.' He held up his hands defensively. 'I admit my conversation was far too serious while we're eating. But the escargot really is excellent,' he added self-derisively. 'Would you like to try one, Leonie?' He held up his fork, with the snail firmly speared on the prongs, enticingly in front of her.

No, she would not. Snails, even cooked in garlic to

hide the fact that was what they were, had never appealed to her. But, then…she didn't doubt that Luke already knew that—which was the precise reason he was offering her one!

She held his gaze for several seconds, knowing he had turned his laughter around on her. They would see about that!

She leant forward slightly, delicately taking the snail off the fork with her teeth, chewing once, before swallowing hard. Thankfully, she could taste nothing other than the garlic. Although her stomach rebelled slightly at the fact that her brain knew precisely what she had just eaten.

'Wonderful,' she said with complete—and obvious—insincerity.

Luke arched darkly mocking brows. 'Like another one?'

'No, thank you,' she assured him primly before turning to Rachel. A Rachel who had been watching the exchange with amused green eyes… 'I really am sorry about the weekend.' Leonie deliberately changed the subject. 'But it will give me a chance this next week to read through the diaries.'

'Make sure you're alone when you do,' Luke advised dryly, continuing to eat his snails himself. 'My mother assures me she had an uproarious time when she first went to Hollywood, and I would hate for anyone to see your blushes!'

'Of course I will be alone when I read them,' Leonie answered tartly. 'As I have assured Rachel, anything she gives me, or tells me, is completely in confidence at this stage.' Although she knew Luke had been half joking in his remark, there had been an underlying element of seriousness in the warning, and she deeply resented the fact that he might doubt her integrity.

'What about later?' Luke challenged, confirming that he had indeed been serious in his warning. 'Can Rachel rely on your—discretion, if you should read or discover anything she would rather didn't go into the book?'

'Of course.' Leonie gave up all idea of finishing her first course, placing her knife and fork down beside the half-eaten food as she met Luke's hard gaze unflinchingly. 'This is, after all, Rachel's book; I'm merely the person filling in the blanks.'

'You—'

'Darling, I trust Leonie implicitly,' Rachel assured her son huskily, giving Leonie a reassuring smile before turning back to Luke. 'Let's just enjoy our meal, hmm,' she encouraged him lightly.

Which, on the surface of things, was exactly what the three of them did during the next couple of hours, the conversation becoming more general after that. But that Luke still didn't trust Leonie, or this biography, was more than obvious. To her, at least...

But she was also well aware that there was nothing she could do or say at this stage that would reassure him. Only the fullness of time, and the finished biography, would be able to do that...

'Thank you for these,' Leonie told Rachel in the hotel suite three hours later as she prepared to take her leave, the briefcase full of diaries held securely in her hand. 'I promise I'll take very good care of them,' she added for the benefit of the brooding Luke as he stood across the room watching them with enigmatic green eyes.

'I'll drive you home,' he offered abruptly even as he moved to join her by the door.

'I drove myself here,' Leonie instantly refused; she had been very conscious of the fact that she had driven here in her own car this evening, refusing any more champagne after that first glass, to move on to mineral water. A fact Luke, she was sure, was well aware of; not much was missed by that razor-sharp gaze.

'In that case, I'll walk you down to your car,' he insisted firmly. 'It's almost midnight,' he rasped as she would have refused a second time.

'I am not Cinderella!' Leonie snapped back resentfully, fully aware that she was going to lose this particular argument—but refusing to do it gracefully. As far as she was concerned, Luke was far too keen on having his own way!

'And I'm not Prince Charming!' Luke came back as sharply.

Leonie turned to look at Rachel as the older woman gave a choking sound, her own sense of humour returning as she saw the laughter glowing in those bright green eyes, Rachel obviously trying very hard to stop herself from laughing.

It was a battle she was destined to lose!

In fact, Rachel laughed so long and so hard, there were tears streaming down her face, and she had to put a hand on the wall to support herself.

'Was it something I said?' Luke mused dryly as Leonie also began to laugh.

'Oh, Luke!' Rachel reached up to cradle his face in both her hands. 'You are priceless!' She kissed him warmly on both cheeks.

'But certainly *not* Prince Charming!' Leonie chuckled.

'No,' Rachel agreed wryly. 'But he has been the love of my life for the last thirty-seven years,' she added seriously, that love shining brightly in her eyes now as she looked proudly up at her son she so obviously adored. 'There have been so many times when I don't know what I would have done without him.'

Leonie shifted uncomfortably, feeling like an intruder, as if Rachel's conversation were for Luke alone. As, indeed, she was sure it was…

Luke returned his mother's gaze intently, searchingly. 'The feeling is reciprocated,' he told her huskily.

Rachel held his gaze for several long seconds before stepping back, smiling brightly. 'Run along now, darlings; some of us need our beauty sleep if we have to start filming in three weeks' time; television can be just too honest at times!' She was once again the glamorously assured actress who had ruled screen and stage for over fifty years.

'You're already far too beautiful to play Elizabeth the first,' Luke assured her. 'From all accounts she had a face like the back end of a bus!'

Rachel laughed softly. 'Not when I play her, darling,' she drawled dryly.

Luke smiled. 'Probably not. I'll call you tomorrow, hmm?' he added gently.

'Fine.' Rachel nodded dismissively before turning to Leonie. 'Have a lovely time at your parents' party tomorrow evening,' she said warmly.

Leonie shot Luke a questioning look as he took the briefcase from her hand as they walked down the hotel corridor together towards the lift, but she could read nothing of his thoughts from his grim expression.

'My car is just parked outside,' she told him huskily as they stepped out into the reception area together, moving to reclaim the briefcase.

'I said I'll walk you to your car,' he bit out tersely.
'Luke—'

'Independence in a woman is admirable,' he rasped
harshly. 'Stubborn stupidity is something else entirely!'

Leonie felt the two wings of angry, embarrassed colour that instantly warmed her cheeks—and she wasn't
sure which emotion was predominant!

Luke looked down at her with mockingly raised
brows. 'Silence in a woman is also something to be
admired,' he drawled derisively.

She glared at him, glad she had worn the high-heeled
sandals now as she found herself only a few inches
shorter than Luke's own considerable height. On her
evenings out with Jeremy, only five feet ten himself,
she always wore flatter-heeled shoes so that she didn't
tower over him; but there was no danger of that with
Luke. And with this man, she had quickly learnt, she
needed every advantage she could get!

She drew in a harsh breath. 'You—'

'Even when it never lasts very long,' he added dryly,
those green eyes openly laughing at her now.

Was there any way to win a verbal battle with this
man? Leonie wondered as she turned and strode forcefully towards the revolving door that led out of the
hotel, all the time aware that Luke was following behind her at a much more leisurely pace. She had tried
returning sarcasm with sarcasm, reasoning with him, or
just ignoring his taunts, but somehow she didn't feel
she had emerged the victor in any of these encounters.

Whether it was just lack of attention because of her
angry preoccupation with Luke, or the unaccustomed
high heels on her sandals, Leonie was never afterwards
sure. All she was aware of was completely losing her

balance, of Luke's cry of alarm as she pitched side-ways, before falling hard onto the pavement outside, the sudden pain in her left ankle making her feel sick.

'What the—?' Luke was at her side in seconds, the doorman quickly joining him, both men endeavouring to raise Leonie to a sitting position.

The shock of finding herself on the pavement instead of on her own two feet was quickly receding, embarrassment quickly taking its place. 'I'm fine.' She pushed away their supporting hands feeling utterly foolish as several other people, in the process of leaving the hotel, turned to stare at her. It was obvious from their amused or disgusted glances that they were attributing her prostration to something other than a mere fall! 'Really,' she assured the two men tartly, attempting to get back onto her feet unaided.

Luke, as she might have known, refused to be dismissed, his arm about her waist as he helped her to stand up.

In truth, Leonie was grateful for his help, her left ankle proving extremely painful when she attempted to put any weight on it.

'Lean on me,' he ordered grimly, his arm like a steel band about her waist as she had no other choice than to do exactly that, her left ankle unable to support her for the moment.

'How stupid of me,' Leonie muttered angrily.

'I'll order a taxi for you,' the doorman offered worriedly.

'I—'

'We have our car here,' Luke arrogantly assured the other man, looking across to where Leonie's car was conspicuously parked beside the hotel. 'Perhaps if you could carry the briefcase for me…?' he added less harshly, bending down to easily lift Leonie up into his arms.

'Of course, sir.' The doorman was only too happy to oblige.

He probably wanted to get her off the forecourt of the hotel, Leonie acknowledged self-disgustedly as Luke walked along with her in his arms as if she weighed nothing at all, unable to even glance at him in her acute embarrassment.

'Thanks,' Luke tersely dismissed the other man once they had reached the car and he was able to put Leonie down, holding out his hand now for Leonie to give him her car keys. 'I'm driving,' he announced in a tone that brooked absolutely no argument.

Leonie, leaning on the bonnet of the car, looked at the car and then back to Luke. 'You'll never fit in it,' she said doubtfully.

'I will with the roof down,' he assured her dryly, unlocking the car with the keys she had given him. 'I had the older model of this car when I was a student,' he added dryly as Leonie continued to look sceptical. 'It will be a bit breezy with the roof down, but I will fit in. Besides,' he added as she would have continued to argue, 'I doubt you're capable of driving yourself…?'

She wasn't. They both knew that she wasn't. But even so… 'I could always get a taxi home,' she told him stubbornly.

'You aren't going straight home,' Luke said grimly even as he opened the passenger door and helped her to get inside. 'You need to have that ankle X-rayed—'

'It's only sprained—'

'I thought your doctorate was in History?' Luke challenged as he straightened.

Her mouth firmed as she instantly got his point. 'It is. But—'

'I'm sure you're right about the sprain, Leonie.' Luke's voice had gentled as he deftly dealt with putting the roof down and sliding the driver's seat all the way back so that it would accommodate his length. 'But I don't think it will do any harm to have it X-rayed, anyway. Okay?' He turned to her, having, as he had claimed he could, managed to get in behind the wheel of her car.

'Okay,' she agreed unhappily, knowing, with Luke behind the driving wheel, that she didn't have any choice in where he chose to take her. In fact, she was surprised he had bothered to consult her at all!

'Cheer up, Leonie; I'm really quite a good driver!' He reached over and squeezed her hand reassuringly, before turning on the ignition, putting the car in gear, and driving them away from the hotel.

He was enjoying himself, Leonie realised after a few minutes, watching him surreptitiously beneath lowered lashes; his eyes gleamed with pleasure, a wolfish grin curving those sculptured lips as he manoeuvred the little car in and out of the traffic.

He was also right about it being 'a bit breezy', Leonie acknowledged with a shiver, desperately trying to sink down lower in the seat so that she didn't feel so much of the cold wind whistling about her bare shoulders. After all, it was only May. May in England to boot.

'Are you cold?' Luke glanced at her, seeming to sense her discomfort, not even waiting for her answer before pulling the car over to the side of the road, completely unconcerned by the other drivers as a couple of them tooted their car horns at them. 'Here.' He began to shrug out of his jacket.

'I couldn't—'

'I thought we had already discussed your unnecessary stubbornness, Leonie?' he reminded grimly, leaning over to drape the black jacket about her shoulders. 'There.' He nodded his satisfaction. 'Is that better?'

Leonie had to admit—to herself, at least!—that it was infinitely warmer snuggled inside Luke's over-big jacket. But the black material also carried the essence of the man with it, the smell of his tangy aftershave, the warmth of his body…!

'Now you're going to be the one that's cold,' she muttered ungratefully.

'I can take it.' Luke shrugged dismissively, his attention distracted as he manoeuvred the car back into the flow of traffic.

The inference being that she couldn't. But…it was much warmer enfolded in his jacket, and she would be a fool to claim otherwise. And Luke had already made his views clear on female foolishness this evening too!

Thank goodness she wouldn't be seeing any more of him this weekend. She—

'Oh, no…!' she groaned as a sudden realisation hit her.

Luke glanced at her sharply. 'What is it?'

'I've just realised—my parents' anniversary party tomorrow.' She grimaced frustratedly. 'I know it's a surprise party, but even so, I don't think it's going to look very good if their only child isn't even there!'

'Of course you'll be there,' Luke dismissed impatiently.

Leonie turned to him frowningly, shaking her head. 'I don't think I'll be able to—'

'I'll drive you to Devon, of course,' Luke cut in dismissively.

'You'll—? No.' She gave a firm shake of her head, horrified at the suggestion. 'I don't think so. Thank you,' she added belatedly.

'Don't be ridiculous, Leonie,' Luke told her tersely. 'Even if that ankle isn't broken, it's still going to be sore for a few days. Too sore for you to be able to drive.'

Leonie's eyes were wide at the thought of Luke driving her anywhere tomorrow, let alone to her grandfather's house in Devon. 'It's very—kind, of you to offer, Luke—' she swallowed hard as she saw the way his mouth twisted derisively at her hesitation over the word 'kind' being applied to him '—but I really don't think that would be—'

'Look, Leonie, you're right about your parents being disappointed if you don't turn up for their party. Even once you've explained about your sprained ankle. Fortunately, I don't have any other plans for this weekend—'

'What about Rachel?' Leonie put in hastily.

His mouth twisted. 'My mother certainly doesn't need me to babysit her when she's in London! She's meeting up with friends over the weekend,' he added impatiently as Leonie continued to look doubtful.

As in Michael Harris? Leonie couldn't help wondering...

'Or is it that you think, in the circumstances, you might take the boyfriend, after all?' Luke rasped harshly.

'His name is Jeremy.' She felt stung in defending. 'And, no, I hadn't thought of asking him...' Especially now, when she was so unsure about that relationship.

She had played with the idea a month or so ago when her grandfather had told her about tomorrow's party, of asking Jeremy to accompany her and so introducing him to her family, but had finally dismissed the idea on the basis that it might give Jeremy the impression she was trying to put their relationship on a more serious level. Now she was grateful she had made that decision...

'Fine,' Luke bit out tersely. 'I'm available, I've offered to drive you—so where is your problem?' he asked harshly, obviously impatient now with her continued protests.

Her problem was this man himself! What on earth were people going to think, her parents, her grandfather, the other family members who would be present at the party tomorrow evening, if she arrived with Luke Richmond as her partner, rather than Jeremy, whom they all vaguely knew she had been dating for the last few months?

No, she couldn't do it!

Could she...?

CHAPTER NINE

'YOU'RE a little early—Jeremy!' Leonie gasped her dismay as, having opened the door to her basement apartment fully, she recognised her visitor, not Luke as she had imagined, but Jeremy.

He gave her a quizzical look as she continued to stare at him. 'I'm not interrupting anything, am I...?'

She gave herself a mental shake. 'No, of course not. I just—I wasn't expecting you,' she awkwardly excused her unwelcoming behaviour. 'Er—would you like to come in?' she offered abruptly.

What on earth was Jeremy doing here on a Saturday afternoon? He hadn't mentioned anything about calling round today when Leonie had telephoned him mid-week and explained she couldn't meet him yesterday evening. In fact, he had never just called round like this before...

'If it's no trouble.' Jeremy shrugged ruefully. 'I—what have you done to your ankle?' He frowned concernedly as Leonie moved back to let him in and he obviously saw the support bandage on her left ankle above the bareness of her foot.

'It's nothing,' Leonie assured him as she led the way through to her sitting-room. 'I slipped last night and gave my ankle a bad sprain.'

A fact the midnight visit to the hospital had confirmed. But the doctor had insisted she wear the support bandage, and stay off her ankle as much as possible, until it felt easier to walk on. Much to Luke's satisfaction!

Luke! She remembered with an anxious glance towards the clock that stood on her unlit fireplace.

She might not have been expecting Jeremy a few minutes ago, but she was expecting Luke to arrive in the next twenty minutes or so in order to drive her to her grandfather's house. The last thing she wanted was for these two men to meet!

She gave Jeremy a bright smile. 'What can I do for you?'

'I'm not sure.' He looked a little uncomfortable, hands thrust into the back pockets of his faded denims. 'You seemed a little—distant, on Monday evening, and I just—Leonie, I haven't done, or said, anything to upset you, have I?' He frowned across at her.

'Of course not.' She forced lightness into her tone; after all, it wasn't Jeremy's fault she felt so uncertain about the continuation of their relationship. That, she knew, was entirely due to Luke! 'I'm just a bit—preoccupied, with this Rachel Richmond biography at the moment,' she dismissed ruefully. 'I did try to warn you at the beginning that it would take up a lot of my time.' She grimaced, at the same time giving another surreptitious glance at the clock.

Almost four o'clock, the time Luke had told her he would arrive to pick her up in order to drive her to Devon. Thankfully, in his own car this time. A three-hour drive, with the roof of Leonie's car down to accommodate Luke's height, had not appealed to either of them!

'Actually, I'm really rather busy this afternoon too,' Leonie continued with a pointed look at the diaries she had spread out on the dining-table as she worked her way through them. So far she had got as far as Rachel's twenty-fifth birthday. 'As you can see,' she added lightly.

Jeremy strolled over to pick up one of the diaries, glancing down at the flowery scrawl that filled the pages, before looking incredulously at Leonie. 'Are these what I think they are?'

Leonie moved the short distance between them to take the diary out of his hand, filled with a sudden, fierce protectiveness. She very much doubted that anyone other than Rachel and herself had ever read these diaries; Luke's comments last night had certainly seemed to indicate that he had never read any of them.

'They are,' Leonie confirmed tersely, placing the diary back on the table with the others. 'I really am rather busy today, Jeremy…' she added pointedly, smiling to take any sharpness out of her words.

'I can see that.' He nodded good-naturedly. 'Are we still okay for Monday evening? The ballet,' he lightly reminded as Leonie looked at him blankly.

'Of course,' she confirmed breathlessly. The ballet! She had totally forgotten that they had booked the seats for *Swan Lake* weeks ago. At the time she had seen it as a promise of the continuation of their relationship; now she could only see it as an enforced evening in Jeremy's company. 'I'm looking forward to it.'

'Good.' Jeremy nodded his satisfaction. 'I'll leave you to get on, then.' He turned to leave, and then paused. 'Have you read the diary yet from the year before her son was born?' he prompted speculatively.

Leonie frowned her irritation with his obvious curiosity. It didn't need a mind-reader to know the reason Jeremy had questioned that particular diary. He was curious, as were a lot of other people, to know who

Luke's father had been. Or still was… The chances were that the man was still alive.

'I'm reading them in order,' she told Jeremy stiffly. 'I haven't got that far yet.'

Jeremy shook his head incredulously. 'It's the first one I would have gone for!'

'Really?' Leonie bit out sharply, finding herself deeply resentful—whether on Rachel's behalf, or Luke's, she wasn't sure—of Jeremy's lascivious interest in who Rachel's lover had been thirty-eight years ago. 'I'm approaching this in a methodical way.' She shrugged dismissively.

Jeremy gave her a teasing look. 'You're not even the least bit curious?'

Of course she was curious, she wouldn't be human if she weren't. But reading the diaries at all felt intrusive on her part, let alone rushing to read that particular diary. Somehow, that felt disloyal to Luke…

'It may not even be in there, Jeremy,' she dismissed, deliberately walking—hobbling?—him towards the door in an effort to get him to leave; the minutes to four o'clock were fast ticking by!

'If you need any help reading through them… Only joking, Leonie.' Jeremy laughed softly at her grim expression, bending to kiss her lightly on the lips. 'See you on Monday.'

Leonie closed the door behind him with firm sharpness, intensely irritated by what he called his 'joking' remarks.

Of course she realised that Rachel's diary from thirty-eight years ago was probably amongst the dozens she still hadn't read, but Leonie had found she really had no desire to read that particular one. No matter how she tried to approach looking at it, professionally or personally, it did somehow feel disloyal to Luke...

Oh, she knew he was arrogant, bossy, sarcastic, downright rude on occasion, but she also knew from his treatment of her last night after she had twisted her ankle that he could be kind, tender, and gently caring if the situation warranted it.

He had taken her to the hospital with the minimum amount of fuss, sat with her while she'd been examined and X-rayed, listened intently to the doctor when he'd come back with the results of those X-rays, driven her home, before helping her to get down the steps to her apartment. He had even offered to help her get undressed and into bed!

An offer she'd had no hesitation in refusing—even if it had taken her twice as long as usual to undress once she'd been on her own, every movement seeming to cause renewed pain to her ankle.

As for Luke's offer to drive her to Devon today...

Personally, she was sure, the less time she spent in Luke's company, the better it would be for her already troubled peace of mind. But from her parents' point of view...they would be deeply disappointed if she weren't at her grandfather's with the rest of the family this evening to help them celebrate their wedding anniversary. Quite what she was going to do with Luke once the two of them had arrived, she wasn't sure, but she would have to cross that bridge when she came to it!

She—

Luke, she realised as the doorbell rang for the second time in ten minutes. A little early, but not as early as she had at first thought!

Her breath caught in her throat as she opened the

door to him. His dark hair was still damp from his shower, the green of his shirt deepened the colour of his eyes, black trousers fitted low down on his hips. Leonie gave an inward groan. How on earth, with her senses reeling just from looking at him, was she supposed to spend the weekend with this man without, at some point, making a complete idiot of herself?

She had no idea, Leonie admitted weakly, but—

'No wonder you ended up flat on your face in those high heels last night; you probably have to wear flat shoes most of the time when you go out with the dwarf!' Luke rasped disparagingly as he walked straight past her into the apartment without waiting for an invitation.

That was how, Leonie acknowledged irritably as she turned to watch him as he strode arrogantly down the hallway to her sitting-room. Luke only had to open his mouth to—

His words implied he had seen Jeremy leaving! Had Jeremy also seen him arriving...?

'Don't look so worried, Leonie,' Luke taunted after she had slowly joined him in the sitting-room. 'I thought it prudent to let the boyfriend leave before I got out of my car and came down here!'

Prudent? Or better ammunition with which to mock her? Knowing Luke, it was the latter.

'For your information, Jeremy is five feet ten inches tall—hardly a dwarf,' she snapped, her head going back challengingly. 'And you needn't have bothered waiting until Jeremy had left. I'm sure he would have enjoyed meeting you,' she added truthfully; Jeremy had shown in the last ten minutes that he was just as curious as the rest of the world when it came to the Richmond family.

Luke's mouth twisted derisively. 'The feeling wouldn't have been reciprocated,' he dismissed tersely before looking around the untidiness of the room, and then glancing down pointedly at her bare feet. 'Are you ready to go?' he drawled sceptically.

Leonie drew in a deeply controlling breath; there was no point in falling out with him before they had even started the journey! 'I just have to get my overnight bag from the bedroom. I can't get a shoe on that foot,' she added in a disgruntled voice as he gave another pointed look at her bare feet.

'Fine,' he sighed impatiently. 'I'll just have to carry you upstairs again then, won't I?'

Leonie gave a pained frown at his obvious terseness. 'Luke,' she began slowly, 'if you've changed your mind about driving me to Devon—'

'I haven't,' he snapped, eyes flashing icy green.

She swallowed hard. 'Then why are you so—irritable?' she said for want of a better word. So much for her deciding a few minutes ago that Luke could be 'kind, tender, and gently caring'!

'I'm not irritable, Leonie—I'm furiously angry!' he bit out forcefully, his hands clenched at his sides.

Leonie looked at him frowningly, totally taken aback by the fierceness of this verbal attack. There was a nerve pulsing in Luke's cheek, his mouth was a thin, angry line, those green eyes so pale they shimmered silver.

'But why...?' She shook her head uncomprehendingly.

'How long had the ageing hippie been here before I arrived?' Luke snapped coldly. 'Or did you telephone him as soon as I left you last night, and he came rushing over to be at your side?'

'Luke—'

'"Luke" nothing!' he rasped furiously, moving forward to pull her roughly into his arms, his mouth coming down forcefully onto hers.

Leonie was so taken aback by the suddenness of his kiss that at first she stood acquiescent in his arms, arms that were wrapped tightly around her.

But the stupefaction didn't last long under the assault of that insulting kiss, Leonie starting to struggle in his arms, pushing against the hardness of his chest.

He wrenched his mouth from hers, looking down at her intently as his hands cradled each side of her face, her cheeks hot against those hands. 'Don't, Leonie!' he groaned throatily before his lips claimed hers for a second time.

But gently this time, sipping from her lips, sensuously searching, asking for her response rather than demanding it.

It was a response Leonie was powerless to resist…

She felt as if she were burning, her body on fire, her skin so sensitive that each touch of Luke's hands was like a searing flame.

His hair, beneath her fingers, felt like liquid silk, dark and soft, Luke groaning low in his throat as she caressed the nape of his neck, teeth gently biting her lips now as desire rose unchecked.

Her nails dug briefly into his skin before her arm moved compulsively about his neck, returning the passion of his kiss, never wanting the pleasure to stop, unsure now where she began and Luke stopped, their bodies curved perfectly into one.

Luke's lips were burning a trail down her throat now, her head back as lips and tongue explored the hollows at the base of her neck, one of his hands moving to cup the tautness of her breast.

Leonie groaned low in her throat as the soft pad of his thumb brushed the turgid nipple, pleasure coursing through her body to centre achingly between her thighs.

She turned her lips to kiss the hardness of his jaw, the smooth planes of his cheeks, his eyes closed as she looked at him, dark lashes fanning cheeks flushed with desire.

She—

'Ouch!' Leonie gave an involuntary groan as she had moved slightly and pain shot through her injured ankle.

Luke's head reared up as he looked down at her concernedly. 'What is it? Did I hurt you?' He held her slightly away from him, his gaze moving searchingly over her body.

Leonie swallowed hard, the sensual spell broken as the full realisation of exactly what she had been doing washed over her. 'I—my ankle hurt.' She couldn't look at him now, overcome with embarrassment at her own response, deliberately moving away from him, able to breathe easier once out of Luke's arms.

If not her ankle, would they have—? Could she have—? Only too easily, she acknowledged with an inward groan.

'What are you thinking now?' Luke rasped hardly, his gaze darkly unfathomable as Leonie finally looked over at him, his expression enigmatic, his jaw tightly clenched.

She wasn't about to tell him what she had been thinking! She didn't even want to think about that herself!

Her chin rose defensively. 'I was thinking that you

still didn't tell me why you were so angry when you arrived,' she answered tautly.

His mouth twisted derisively, whether at himself, or her, Leonie couldn't tell. 'Oh, I told you, Leonie—you just weren't listening!'

Her eyes widened in puzzlement. 'But—'

'Shouldn't we be going, Leonie?' Luke gave a pointed look at his plain gold wrist-watch. 'It's after four already.'

And whose fault was that? she inwardly chuntered to herself at the injustice of the accusation in his voice. 'You still want to drive me?'

'I still want to drive you,' he echoed dryly. 'Your bag is in the bedroom, you said?'

'Yes, but—Luke—!' She stopped him as he would have turned and left the room. 'You don't know where my bedroom is,' she said lamely when he turned back to her, his brows raised with obvious impatience.

He grimaced derisively. 'The apartment isn't that big that it will take me long to find it!' he mocked, then he paused before leaving the room. 'Or is it something else about my going into your bedroom that bothers you?' His gaze narrowed speculatively.

Leonie frowned. It seemed far too intimate to have him go to her bedroom, yes—which, after what had happened between them a few minutes ago, seemed rather ridiculous of her! But other than that, she couldn't think—

'Perhaps you haven't made the bed yet?' Luke added with hard derision.

Colour blazed in her cheeks at the clear insult in his accusation. 'For your information, Jeremy only arrived ten minutes before you did!' she snapped resentfully.

Luke gave a humourless smile. 'What a pity!' he muttered with complete insincerity.

How was it possible to go from burning passion, to burning anger, in just a few seconds? Leonie had no idea—she just knew that only Luke was capable of inducing those two strong emotions within her in such quick succession. In fact, at all!

She drew in a controlling breath, determined not to give him the satisfaction of losing her temper with him. 'As we've just proved,' she bit out scornfully, 'my ankle isn't up to passion at the moment!' She met his gaze challengingly, refusing to confirm or deny his suppositions concerning her relationship with Jeremy. Let him think what he liked—he usually did, anyway!

Luke's eyes were once again that transparent green of a cat's. 'I trust you didn't let your boyfriend look at those?' He nodded abruptly in the direction of the diaries that lay spread over the table. 'After all, my mother may not mind you reading them, but I don't think she intended them for anyone else's eyes!'

'Of course Jeremy hasn't read them!' Leonie hurried over to tidy up the diaries, bright wings of guilty colour in her cheeks as she put them back inside the briefcase, seeing all too clearly inside her head the image of Jeremy picking up one of the diaries. But he hadn't had a chance to actually read anything that was written there. Had he…?

'You don't sound too sure…?' Luke rasped harshly.

Her eyes flashed deeply grey as she raised her head to glare across the room at him. 'Of course I'm sure,' she snapped angrily, closing the lid of the briefcase with a decisive click before locking it. 'Now, as you've already pointed out, Luke, it's getting late, and I don't think it will be much of a surprise for my parents if I arrive *after* the party has started!'

Luke continued to look at her speculatively for several long seconds before giving a sharp inclination of his head and turning to abruptly leave the room.

Leonie's breath left her lungs in a shaky sigh—the first sign she had that she had actually been holding her breath at all!

She had no idea how this happened, how it kept happening, but being around Luke was like being around a keg of dynamite—with no idea when, or if, it was going to explode in her face!

The weekend ahead of her, with Luke as her obvious escort, seemed even less appealing than it had before…

CHAPTER TEN

'TIME to put your best foot forward, Leonie. Oops, sorry, I forgot—at the moment you only have one best foot!' Luke drawled mockingly as he slid out from behind the driving wheel of his car to stand on her grandfather's driveway, flexing his tired back muscles as he did so.

Leonie made no effort to open the door on her own side of the vehicle, taking a few seconds to breathe deeply, all the time telling herself to just ignore him, that Luke was deliberately trying to annoy her.

As he had been doing for most of the drive down here. Baiting her more aptly described it, and after three hours of his biting sarcasm she was ready to hit him. Except, she wouldn't give him the satisfaction!

'Come on, Leonie.' Luke impatiently opened the door beside her. 'You said your parents were due to arrive at seven-thirty, which is in fifteen minutes or so, and you still have to go inside and make yourself look beautiful,' he added derisively.

She bit her lip to stop her sharp retort this time, the stinging pain at least taking her mind off her throbbing ankle after three hours in a car, if it couldn't stop her rising anger towards Luke.

She wordlessly swung her legs out of the car, her left ankle throbbing painfully as she did so, visibly swollen beneath the support bandage.

Luke's expression darkened as he looked down at her ankle. 'Why the hell didn't you tell me?' he rasped,

125

going down on his haunches to better inspect her swollen limb, although he wisely didn't actually touch it.

'What good would it have done?' Leonie shrugged dismissively.

Luke's expression was dark as he looked up at her. 'I could have stopped the car and helped you onto the back seat for one thing,' he snapped impatiently. 'You could have had your foot elevated then.'

She hadn't thought of that. But, in truth, Luke's behaviour on the drive here had been so unreasonable, his sarcasm so deeply biting, that her pride wouldn't have let her ask him to help her even if she had thought of it.

'It doesn't matter,' she dismissed, moving to the edge of the car seat in preparation of standing up. 'You'll have to move your car down the lane beside the cottage with the others, I'm afraid, so that my parents don't see them.' She grimaced, noticing the twitching of curtains inside her grandfather's cottage as the family obviously waited to surprise her parents.

'In a minute,' Luke bit out grimly, bending down to swing her up into his arms.

'What are you doing?' Leonie squealed, very conscious of those twitching curtains as Luke cradled her against his chest before straightening to walk towards the front door.

Luke looked down at her with obvious irritation. 'Don't be ridiculous, Leonie; you know you aren't able to walk on that ankle!'

No, she probably wasn't—but she would have given it a good try, rather than have the majority of her close family see her being carried into the cottage by a handsome stranger!

'Leonie!' Her grandfather opened the cottage door,

frowning his concern. 'Luke…?' he realised belatedly. 'What on earth—?'

'A sprained ankle,' Luke explained economically. 'Do you think we could come inside, Leo?' he drawled wryly. 'She may appear small, but I can assure you your granddaughter weighs a lot more than she looks!'

Luke… Leo… Of course, these two men had met before, when Luke had been researching the possibility of writing a screenplay of her grandfather's exploits during the war! She had completely forgotten that fact during these last few hours of being subjected to Luke's biting sarcasm…

As for Luke's remarks about her weight…! 'You're the one who insisted on carrying me,' she snapped irritably.

Luke's eyes gleamed with laughter as he looked briefly down at her. 'Over the threshold, too,' he taunted even as he stepped into her grandfather's cottage.

'Very funny,' Leonie muttered, that embarrassed colour back in her cheeks.

'Where shall I put her?' Luke turned to her grandfather.

Just as if she were a sack of potatoes, Leonie thought disgruntedly. Why not? Luke seemed to be implying she weighed as much as one!

'The rest of the family are through here.' Her slightly dazed grandfather opened the door for them off the hallway that led into his sitting-room.

Ordinarily this was a large, sunny room, extending the full length of the cottage, but with twenty or so family members already congregated there the room looked much smaller. It also brought Leonie, still cradled in Luke's arms, straight into the midst of her obviously already curious family!

Not that Luke seemed at all thrown by the twenty pairs of eyes suddenly levelled on him, heading straight for the sofa in front of the window, bending slightly before lowering Leonie onto its length.

He straightened with obvious relief at having relinquished his burden, turning to shake her grandfather's hand. 'It's good to see you again,' he told the older man warmly.

'And you.' Her grandfather still looked slightly dazed by the unexpected visitor who had accompanied Leonie.

'Luke very kindly offered to drive me down here when I sprained my ankle,' Leonie put in lightly, her gaze steadily meeting Luke's as he turned to give her a mocking glance.

'Kind' didn't quite describe the way he had behaved towards her on the drive down here—and they both knew it! But she could hardly say that, could she? Besides, whatever his behaviour, Luke *had* driven her here, and that was the important thing.

'Mummy and Daddy haven't arrived yet, have they?' She frowned worriedly.

'Er—no, not yet.' Her grandfather still seemed dazed. 'You mentioned that you and Luke had met, Leonie, but you didn't say—didn't say—well—' He looked lost for words.

Luke chuckled softly at the older man's obvious discomfort. 'Don't worry about it, Leo.' He squeezed the other man's shoulder reassuringly. 'I'll explain later. In the meantime, Leonie and I need to change our clothes before the guests of honour arrive…?'

'Of course.' Her grandfather seemed relieved to have

something positive to focus on. 'Can you manage the stairs, Leonie?'

'Only if I carry her,' Luke answered dryly before Leonie had chance to make a reply. 'Which I'm quite happy to do,' he added derisively.

Which, at this precise moment, Leonie was quite happy to let him do, too! Her family seemed to have got over their surprise, chatting amongst themselves now in lowered tones. Although, as she knew from experience, they wouldn't be able to contain their curiosity for much longer. In fact, she could see her great-uncle Tom, the widower of one of her grandfather's younger sisters, already on his way over here. No doubt he had been chosen by the tacit agreement of the rest of the family to find out what he could about Leonie's friend.

'We'll need the bags from the car,' she reminded Luke as he swung her back up into his arms. 'Hello, Uncle Tom, I'll see you in a few minutes,' she called over Luke's shoulder as he turned to leave the room. 'I'll introduce you to everyone later,' she told Luke firmly as he seemed to hesitate.

His face was expressionless as he paused in the hall-way to look down at her. 'Would you prefer me to leave? I could always come back tomorrow and drive you back to London?'

Much as she might feel tempted to accept his offer, she knew she couldn't do it; it would be the height of bad manners after he had taken the trouble to drive her here.

'Don't be silly,' she dismissed awkwardly. 'Unless you would rather not stay?' The thought had suddenly occurred to her. After all, driving her here was one thing, having to fend off the curiosity of her family was something else entirely—and Luke might just have become aware of that himself!

He shrugged. 'I was actually looking forward to talking to your grandfather again,' he admitted ruefully. 'But I don't want to make things awkward for you.'

'You aren't,' Leonie assured him abruptly. 'Grandfather usually puts me in the bedroom to the left at the top of the stairs,' she directed as Luke began their ascent.

Luke quirked darkly mocking brows. 'He's probably wondering right now whether he's expected to ''put me'' in there with you!' he drawled.

That thought had already occurred to Leonie. Oh, not in quite the way Luke had put it, but her grandfather probably did wonder what sleeping arrangements he was supposed to expect for the two of them. She would reassure him about that when she returned downstairs too!

'Possibly,' she allowed tightly as Luke nudged the door open to the low-ceilinged bedroom and placed her on the bed. 'Don't worry, Luke, I'll sort that out with Grandfather later.'

He looked down at her with amused eyes. 'I wasn't worrying, Leonie,' he assured her huskily, looking pointedly at the double bed she sat on. 'That certainly looks big enough for the two of us.'

Her cheeks felt as if they were on fire. 'It may do,' she snapped. 'But even if we were—even if we—'

'Were lovers,' Luke put in helpfully, his tone mocking.

'Yes!' Leonie hissed, glaring up at him. 'Even if that were the case, there is no way I would expect my grandfather to accept the two of us sleeping together here.'

Luke's mouth twisted wryly. 'Believe me, Leonie, if the two of us spent the night in that bed together, we would not be sleeping!' he drawled with amusement.

In light of what had happened between them at her apartment earlier, Leonie did not find this conversation in the least amusing!

She gave him an irritated frown. 'Would you mind getting my bag from the car?'

'Not at all,' he returned tauntingly, green eyes dark with amusement—at her expense. 'I'll move the car, too, while I'm down there. I won't be long,' he assured her, having to duck under the low door frame in order to leave the room without hitting his head.

Leonie was glad of the respite from his company, relaxing the tension from her shoulders. She should have stuck to her decision last night not to let Luke drive her here, should never have let him talk her round.

Because she already knew this weekend, with Luke here, was going to be worse—much worse!—than she could ever have envisaged!

'You don't look like either of them,' Luke remarked softly at her side.

'Sorry?' Leonie turned to him frowningly, having been watching her parents as they moved around the room talking animatedly to the family that had congregated to help them celebrate their anniversary.

Her parents had arrived half an hour ago, been absolutely astonished—or, at least, they had appeared to be astonished—by this surprise party that had been organised in their honour. They had arrived for the weekend with the thought that they were simply going out to dinner with Leonie and her grandfather to celebrate their anniversary. But the fact that Leonie's mother had arrived wearing her best black dress made Leonie wonder if her more astute mother was as surprised as she appeared to be…

'I was just remarking on the fact that if I hadn't already known you're adopted, I probably would have been able to guess as much, anyway; you look absolutely nothing like either of your parents,' Luke said evenly.

It was true that she was adopted. It was also true that not even her colouring, blonde hair and grey eyes, was the same as either of her adoptive parents, her father tall and dark with blue eyes, her mother a petite redhead with brown eyes. But even so…

'How did you know that I'm adopted?' Leonie murmured softly, frowning heavily.

'It was in the book,' Luke answered dismissively, looking around the room at the other guests. 'Your book, Leonie,' he added pointedly, looking down at her now as she still frowned. '"Leo Winston has one son, Richard, and an adopted granddaughter, Leonora." That's you, isn't it?' he prompted gently.

Yes, that was her. She had completely forgotten that footnote in her book. But obviously Luke hadn't…

Luke looked at her searchingly. 'It's the reason you try so hard, isn't it? The reason you became a historian,' he added at her silence. 'To be like your adoptive grandfather.'

Leonie stared at him. How could he possibly have known that?

Luke smiled at her. 'Come on, Leonie, let's get into this party, hmm?' he encouraged lightly. 'We could start by having you introduce me to the rest of the family!'

Her ankle was less swollen now, and her grandfather had found an old stick that he used when he went off on his long country rambles, enabling her to manage the stairs easier on her own, and to get about on her own, too.

'Of course,' she answered distractedly.

Luke took a firm hold of her arm as he guided her across the room to where several of her relatives stood talking together.

But Leonie was still slightly dazed by Luke's casual reference to her adoption.

Her parents had discovered very early on in their marriage that her mother was unable to have children, had adopted baby Leonie when she'd been only a few months old—her mother had felt it would be totally dishonest to adopt a son and heir!—but the adoption was a subject that was never discussed amongst the family, her mother seeing her barrenness as some sort of slight on her part, a slight she never allowed to be discussed. By anyone...

Leonie had felt—much to her mother's displeasure!—when she'd written her grandfather's biography, that it would be equally dishonest not to mention that fact. But having Luke talk about it so casually had totally thrown Leonie. And that he had guessed so easily, it seemed, the real reason for her chosen career...

But she couldn't think about that any more at the moment, had to make the introductions for Luke to her eagerly awaiting family. 'Aunt Trudie, can I introduce you to Luke Richmond? Luke, my great-aunt Trudie, grandfather's younger sister,' she added by way of explanation. 'And this is Uncle Eric. Lastly Uncle Tom.' She smiled warmly at the great-uncle who had always been her favourite amongst the large family.

'Any friend of Leonie's…' Uncle Tom smiled, shaking Luke's hand warmly, as tall as the younger man, his dark hair showing only traces of silver at his temples, despite his seventy-five years.

'I'm afraid that until this moment Leonie has told me absolutely nothing about any of you,' Luke drawled. 'But I'm very pleased to meet you all,' he added lightly.

'Do we hear wedding bells?' Aunt Trudie twinkled speculatively, a lively seventy-year-old who liked nothing better than matchmaking for the numerous younger members of the family.

But at that moment Leonie very much wished she hadn't included her in that number, her cheeks blushing fiery-red at her great-aunt's last comment.

'Only if they're pealing for someone else,' she answered sharply. 'Luke is—a work colleague,' she added firmly. 'Who very kindly offered to drive me here when I hurt my ankle.'

She deliberately didn't look at Luke, knowing he would be questioning the description of 'work colleague'. But she had no intention of letting her family believe there was any romantic connection between the two of them; otherwise Aunt Trudie would have them married off before they had chance to protest!

'That was kind.' Aunt Trudie beamed approvingly at Luke, blue eyes twinkling merrily. 'Although I wouldn't dismiss Luke's kindness as just that if I were you, Leonie,' she added archly. 'After all, it isn't as if he were just driving you round the corner, now is it?'

No, it wasn't, Leonie acknowledged irritably. But this familial teasing was the last thing she felt in the mood for when she was still so shaken by Luke's mention of her adoption. 'Would you all excuse me?' she said brightly. 'I need to check with Grandfather about the cake.' She didn't wait for any of them to reply, turning to limp over to where her grandfather stood talking to her parents.

'Hello, darling.' Her father put his arm about her shoulders and gave her a warm hug. 'You all did incredibly well keeping this a secret from your mother and I.'

'It was Grandfather's idea.' She smiled.

'So kind of you, Leo,' her mother drawled, reaching up to peck her father-in-law coolly on the cheek.

At best it was a perfunctory kiss, but Leonie knew, and accepted, that its coolness was typical, not selective, of her mother.

Leonie had thought, once she was old enough to know of her adoption, that her mother's lack of emotion towards her was because she wasn't really her child, but with maturity Leonie had realised that her mother simply didn't have any emotion to give. To anyone. Which, as Luke seemed to have also guessed, was one of the reasons Leonie had turned to her grandfather for love and approval.

How on earth her father, a warmly loving man, coped with such coldness was beyond her. But, for all that, the marriage had endured for twenty-nine years, so Leonie could only assume her father was happy with things the way they were.

'We should go and talk to Trudie and Eric, Richard,' her mother prompted evenly. 'And Tom, of course,' she added belatedly, a certain coolness back in her voice.

Leonie watched as her father, after kissing her lightly on the cheek, obediently accompanied her mother over to the group where Luke still stood talking to her elderly relatives.

He might be Leonie's favourite relative, but Uncle Tom had certainly never been so with Leonie's mother. Widowed five years ago, his wife having been confined to a wheelchair for most of their married life, Tom had enjoyed a certain freedom these last couple of years after all those years of devotion to Aunt Sally. It was a freedom that Leonie's mother most certainly did not approve of.

'Leonie—'

'Grandfather—'

'You first,' her grandfather invited wryly as they both began talking at the same time.

She grimaced, not absolutely certain what she wanted to say. Or if she really wanted to say anything. Throughout her childhood her grandfather had always been her champion, always there for her. It was silly really, she was no longer a child to need such assurance, but, disturbed as she had been by Luke's earlier conversation, she had once again turned to her grandfather for the emotional support he had always given her.

She glanced across at Luke now as he stood chatting so easily with her parents and assorted elderly relatives. Tall, self-assured, he appeared to be at his charming best this evening—and totally oblivious to how his earlier conversation had unnerved her. In reality, there was absolutely no reason why he should—

Leonie became absolutely still as she now stared across the room, all the colour draining from her cheeks as she did so.

It couldn't be!

She must be imagining it!

But, no…the shape of the head was the same, the way the dark hair fell in soft waves, even the smile, so cynical in Luke at times, was the same…!

Leonie looked about her desperately, sure that everyone must be able to see what she could see, but no one else, including her grandfather, seemed to be staring in the way she was.

Was she the only one who could see the likeness between the two men as they stood so close together? Could no one else see that the two men were so alike they must be related in some way?

But if that were the case—if that were so—

No, it couldn't be, she inwardly protested again, it simply couldn't be!

CHAPTER ELEVEN

'LEONIE, if you don't tell me what's wrong with you I'm going to pull the car over to the side of the road and park there until you do!' Luke's frustrated anger was more than evident in his voice.

Leonie sat huddled on her side of the car, miserably uncommunicative—as she had been in the hours since they'd left her grandfather's house to drive back to London.

It had been the most miserable weekend she had ever spent in her entire life, made more so by having had to keep up a happy front for the sake of her family, the hours having seemed to drag by until she'd been able to make her excuses on Sunday afternoon and leave.

There were so many things she needed to know, so many things she wanted to ask, but the only person she felt able to ask those questions wasn't there to answer them.

Rachel...

Only Rachel, Leonie felt, could tell her what she needed to know. What she half dreaded knowing...!

Did Luke know? Had Rachel talked to him, told him the truth? If she had then Luke must be almost as good an actor as his mother—because not by one single word or gesture during the entire weekend had he revealed that he knew he'd been in the presence of his own father!

Leonie had no idea how it could possibly be, how the two had ever met thirty-eight years ago, but as

Saturday evening had progressed she had become more and more convinced that her suspicion was true. The fact that no one else in the room seemed to have noticed the similarity between the two men seemed absolutely incredible to her, and Leonie desperately needed to talk to Rachel before she did or said anything else. Even to Luke.

Especially to Luke!

'My ankle is a little painful, that's all,' she muttered dismissively.

He gave her a scathing glance. 'All weekend?'

She sighed heavily. 'You seemed to be enjoying yourself well enough on Saturday evening.' After the shock she had received Leonie had spent most of the evening in a daze, but every time she'd glanced at Luke he had been talking and laughing with one member of her family or another.

His mouth was set in a grim line. 'I thought I should make the effort as you were looking so miserable!'

'That isn't fair!' she protested frowningly. 'My parents told me they had a great time.'

'Your grandfather, on the other hand, was very concerned about you,' Luke rasped.

Now that she could perhaps understand. She had been totally dazed after looking across the room and seeing that similarity between the two men, having had to make her excuses to her grandfather and escape into the kitchen for a short time so that she could gather her scattered wits together.

It had taken every ounce of will-power she had to go back and join the party, to keep up the pretence of enjoying herself. And now Luke told her she might as well have saved herself the trouble, because neither he nor her grandfather had been convinced by her act.

'I'm sorry,' she mumbled.

'That's it?' Luke rasped disgustedly. 'You're sorry?'

She turned to glare at him. 'That's it,' she confirmed tightly. 'When does your mother return to Hampshire?'

'When does…? Leonie, we weren't talking about my mother,' he snapped impatiently.

'I was,' she said pointedly.

He drew in an angry breath. 'Some time tomorrow, I believe. But I don't see—'

'Luke, I'm very tired,' she said truthfully, hardly having slept at all the night before, going over and over in her mind the repercussions of what the future would hold for all of them if her suspicion turned out to be correct. 'Would you mind very much if I had a little doze until we get back to London?'

'When you put it like that—no, I wouldn't mind,' he bit out irritably. 'But I think you and I need to talk—'

'Not now, Luke, hmm?' she murmured distantly even as she settled down further into her seat.

'No, not now,' he conceded impatiently, turning his attention frustratedly back to the road.

Leonie watched him for several minutes beneath lowered lashes. Did he know the truth? There was no way of knowing that without revealing what she had guessed herself this weekend. But as it was only a guess—something that seemed more and more fantastic the further they drove away from Devon!—Leonie had no intention of talking to Luke about it until she had at least broached the subject with Rachel.

Although how on earth she was supposed to do that Leonie had no idea! It wasn't something one usually just blurted out over a cup of tea or coffee—oh, by the way, were you and so-and-so lovers thirty-eight years ago?

There was always the diaries, of course. Perhaps, as Jeremy had suggested yesterday, Leonie should read the diary of thirty-eight years ago. Although, in the circumstances, that now seemed like even more of an intrusion than before...

Sleep, Leonie, she instructed herself firmly. There was nothing to be done until after she had spoken to Rachel, and at least if she were asleep she wouldn't have to answer any more of Luke's questions.

The telephone was ringing in her apartment as Leonie unlocked the door, hobbling over to answer it while Luke came in behind with her over-night bag.

'May I speak to Mr Richmond, please?' came the brisk female voice on the other end of the line.

Leonie frowned. Who on earth could be telephoning Luke at her apartment? More to the point, who could possibly know he could be reached here?

'Just a moment.' She put her hand over the mouthpiece before turning to Luke. 'It appears to be for you,' she informed him waspishly.

'Me?' He looked as stunned as she felt.

'You,' Leonie echoed shortly, handing over the receiver. 'I'll go and put my bag in the bedroom while you take the call.' She turned and abruptly left the room.

What a cheek. How dare Luke give her telephone number to some—some woman? Of all the—

'Leonie?' Luke appeared at the bedroom door, his face ashen, his expression bleak. 'I have to go. My mother has collapsed and I have to go to her—'

'I'll come with you.' Leonie was instantly regretful

of her angry thoughts of a few seconds ago. 'Yes, Luke,' she added firmly as he would have spoken.

He gave a rueful grimace. 'I was about to say I would like that, thank you,' he murmured huskily.

'Sorry.' Leonie blushed at her unwarranted sharpness, picking up her handbag in readiness of leaving. 'Did the hospital say what happened?' she prompted concernedly as they walked out to the car.

'It wasn't anyone from a hospital on the telephone,' he told her grimly as he unlocked the car doors for them to get in. 'She said she was Michael Harris's assistant, and that my mother is at his private clinic in Mayfair.'

Michael Harris, the man Leonie had met at dinner the previous weekend at Rachel's house, was a doctor...?

It would explain several things if that were the case: the fact that an emergency had delayed him, his refusal of alcohol with his meal—probably in case he was called back to that same emergency?

But a doctor of what? Obviously one specialised enough to have his own clinic...

It was obvious from Luke's grim expression that until today he hadn't been aware the other man was a doctor, either, so it was no good asking him for information. Besides, he looked too upset at the moment to want to talk about anything, concentrating on his driving to the exclusion of everything else.

Leonie reached over and gently touched his arm. 'It will be all right,' she reassured him warmly, at the same time wondering why she had said that; she had no idea whether this was going to be all right or not! But if wishing made it so, then it would be all right...

Luke gave her a brief, grateful smile. 'I hope that

you didn't mind them calling your apartment? It seems they managed to track me down through your grandfather.'

Who was now probably wondering what on earth was going on too!

'As long as they did find you, nothing else matters,' she assured him. 'What happened, Luke?' she prompted again softly.

Luke swallowed hard. 'I only know that my mother collapsed and was admitted to the clinic two hours ago.' He scowled. 'That damned woman refused to tell me any other details over the telephone, insisted that Michael will be there to meet me when I arrive, and explain everything. But that doesn't help me right now,' he added harshly.

No, it didn't. And Luke was naturally deeply upset, a nerve pulsing in his jaw, only the concentration necessary on the driving, it seemed, keeping him in the least calm.

Which wasn't surprising; he and Rachel were obviously very close, closer even than most mothers and sons, and Rachel was all the family Luke had in the world—

No, that wasn't quite true, Leonie realised slowly, not if what she had guessed over the weekend happened to be true...

Although that did nothing to change the situation now, Leonie told herself firmly. Now they just had to concentrate on Rachel, and hope that whatever was wrong, it wasn't too serious. Although it was obvious from Michael's presence at dinner last weekend that he and Rachel had known each other for some time...

'I'm glad you're with me, Leonie,' Luke told her

gruffly as he turned the car into the driveway of the clinic.

She gave his arm another squeeze as the two of them got out of the car and walked over to the entrance of the clinic. 'I've grown very fond of your mother over the last few weeks.' Even to her own ears the words sounded inadequate, but some of the alternatives were just too over-emotional. Something Luke certainly didn't need from her at the moment.

Although it did magnify in her own mind the realisation that had hit her like a lightning bolt yesterday evening—she was in love with Luke!

She wasn't sure when it had happened, or even how, she simply knew that she was in love with him. Loved him so much, that the lukewarm emotion she had felt towards Jeremy now seemed slightly ridiculous!

Although, much good loving Luke was going to do her…

Falling in love, she had always thought, the realisation of all her hopes and dreams for the future, was going to be the happiest experience of her life. But unrequited love had to be the most painful!

Realising the previous evening that she was in love with Luke had only added to her misery, until today she felt so sunk within it there seemed no way out…

'Luke!' Michael Harris, as promised, was in the reception area to meet them, wearing a formal dark suit, his tie knotted precisely at the throat of his pristine white shirt. He came forward to shake the younger man by the hand, before turning to Leonie. 'Leonie, isn't it…?'

'Michael.' She nodded, shaking his proffered hand. 'How is Rachel?' she prompted quickly, able to sense

Luke's rising tension at this delay in what he obviously considered an exchange of banal pleasantries.

'Stable, I'm happy to say,' Michael reported evenly.

'Just what does that mean?' Luke scorned. 'What the hell happened to her?' he demanded harshly.

The older man grimaced. 'I think it would be better if I left it to your mother to explain—'

'I don't,' Luke rasped, his gaze narrowed grimly on the other man.

Michael sighed regretfully. 'I really can't break patient-doctor confidentiality—'

'That's my mother you have in there,' Luke bit out forcefully, hands clenched at his sides, that nerve pulsing erratically in the rigid line of his jaw.

'I'm aware of that, Luke,' Michael Harris began soothingly.

'Then you must also be aware that I want to know exactly what is wrong with her!' Luke rasped.

Michael turned to Leonie with brows raised, obviously asking for her help.

Although what on earth he expected her to do with Luke in this mood she had no idea! Besides, if the circumstances had been reversed, she would have been asking exactly the same questions as Luke was!

'Luke, perhaps it would be better if we went in to see Rachel first?' she suggested persuasively. 'You can always talk to Michael again afterwards.'

'Yes, that's probably the best thing to do,' Michael quickly agreed, turning to take them through the double doors that led into the clinic, pausing outside one of the doors. 'I should warn you that I've given Rachel something for the pain, and as a consequence she may be a little sleepy,' he said in a hushed whisper. 'I would appreciate it if you don't stay too long.'

'I don't give a damn what you would appreciate!' Luke snapped. 'And what pain are you talking about?' he demanded sharply. 'Michael—' He broke off abruptly as the other man opened the door to his mother's room.

'Rachel, I have two visitors for you.' Michael spoke softly as he entered the room. 'Very welcome visitors, I'm sure.' He smiled confidently as he stepped back to let Leonie and Luke enter the room.

Quite what she had been expecting, Leonie wasn't sure, but Rachel looked as beautiful as ever as she lay back against the pillows in the bed. Slightly pale perhaps, her eyes deeply green against that pallor, but beautiful nonetheless...

'Luke.' She smiled her pleasure at seeing her son walk into the comfortably furnished room. 'And Leonie,' she added with equal warmth, holding out a hand to each of them.

Leonie felt the prick of tears against her lids at Rachel's obvious pleasure in seeing her here too. She realised at that moment that over the last few weeks this woman, still so much a stranger to her in many ways, had come to mean almost as much to Leonie as she now realised Luke did.

'What's going on, Rachel?' Luke was the first to reach his mother's side, tightly gripping the slender hand she held out to him.

'I'll leave you to talk,' Michael put in lightly. 'But don't stay too long, hmm?' he encouraged softly before leaving them alone together.

'Perhaps I should wait outside too—'

'No!' Rachel sharply overrode Leonie's hesitant suggestion. 'Please stay,' she added with an apologetic smile for her abruptness. She held her free hand out to

Leonie. 'It's so good to see you both,' she added emotionally.

On closer inspection, Leonie could see Rachel looked extremely tired, as if all her usual enthusiasm for life had been sucked out of her, and her hand, within Leonie's light grip, felt ethereal, the skin almost appearing translucent.

Leonie glanced across the bed at Luke, could see by the shimmering silver-green of his eyes, the paleness of his cheeks, that he had also noted his mother's sudden frailty.

'Why don't we both sit down, Luke?' Leonie suggested huskily. 'We'll give Rachel a crick in her neck towering over her like this!' she added with forced lightness.

'Yes, do sit down, darlings,' Rachel encouraged with a little of her usual spirit.

'Mother—'

'Luke, I said sit down,' his mother repeated firmly.

To Leonie's surprise he did exactly that, bending his tall frame into the chair beside the bed. Although, in the circumstances, he was hardly likely to argue, was he?

'Do stop scowling, Luke,' Rachel added teasingly. 'It will give you lines!'

He drew in a harsh breath. 'Rachel, try all the delaying tactics you like, but be warned I am not going to wait for ever for an explanation!''

'Such a loving, well-behaved little boy,' Rachel murmured, shaking her head ruefully. 'All right, Luke.' She smiled as he looked ready to explode at this totally unrelated reminiscing. 'I've had some slight chest pains, that's all, and Michael thought it best if I came in here for a few days. For tests and things,' she added uninterestedly.

Luke's eyes narrowed. 'What sort of ''tests and things''?'

'Oh, just the usual, I expect,' his mother dismissed. 'I wonder if you could telephone Janet and ask her—?'

'Rachel!' Luke did explode this time, his expression thunderous. 'What, exactly, is wrong with you?'

'Well, I expect I've had a slight heart attack, darling,' Rachel began lightly.

'You ''expect''—' Luke broke off, releasing Rachel's hand to stand up with barely suppressed violence, glaring down at his mother with narrowed eyes. 'And have you had any of these ''slight heart attacks'' before?' he questioned astutely.

'Actually, no,' Rachel answered him mildly, obviously not in the least perturbed by his anger.

Although she did give Leonie's hand a reassuring squeeze.

But was it reassuring, Leonie suddenly wondered, or a plea for help in handling this delicate situation? Looking at the fine sheen of perspiration that had broken out on the other woman's brow, her increased pallor, obvious signs that this meeting with Luke was having more of an effect on Rachel than she cared to admit, Leonie had a feeling it was the latter.

'Luke,' Leonie began softly, 'I think perhaps we should leave your mother to rest now.'

If anything his expression darkened even more. 'I—'

'Michael did say we weren't to stay too long and tire Rachel,' she reminded gently, knowing she had been right in her conjecture as she felt Rachel's fingers squeeze hers in gratitude for this timely intervention.

Luke looked down intently at his mother. 'Fine,' he finally bit out tersely, obviously not at all happy about leaving, but also seeming to become aware of how much frailer Rachel looked now than when they had arrived a few minutes ago. 'But don't think you've got away with this quite that easily,' he added warningly to his mother. 'I'm coming back later this evening—'

'If Michael will let you,' his mother teased.

'I'll be back,' Luke assured her grimly. 'And when I do I'll expect a full explanation from you.'

Rachel gave a tired laugh. 'I never expected anything else,' she answered affectionately. 'Did the two of you have a lovely weekend?' she added interestedly.

Leonie couldn't help it, her fingers tightened convulsively about the older woman's, and she received a searching look from Rachel at this involuntary response to her casually put question.

One thing Leonie had realised by seeing Rachel weakened like this: it was going to be some time before she dared risk asking the other woman about Luke's father...

'Very nice,' Leonie answered stiltedly, releasing Rachel's hand to stand up. 'I hope you feel better soon,' she added inadequately.

'I'm sure I shall,' Rachel answered her distractedly, seeming aware that Leonie was avoiding meeting her searching gaze. 'I'll see you later, darling.' She gently touched Luke's cheek as he bent down to kiss her. 'Don't give Michael too hard a time, hmm?' she added lightly.

Luke's mouth twisted ruefully at these words of advice. 'I'm sure he's more than capable of dealing with anything I might have to say to him!'

'I'm sure that he is.' Rachel laughed huskily.

'Leonie…?' she called softly as Leonie would have preceded Luke out of the room.

Leonie turned back reluctantly. 'Yes?' She kept her voice deliberately neutral.

Rachel sat up higher against the pillows. 'Could you come back here for a moment?'

'I won't be long,' Leonie assured Luke as he scowled darkly, turning to walk back to the bedside.

Rachel looked up at her intently. 'Did something happen this weekend that I should know about?' She kept her voice low enough so that Luke, standing in the doorway, shouldn't hear what she said.

'To Luke?' Leonie kept her voice equally low. 'No,' she assured the other woman.

'Ah.' Rachel's breath left her in an understanding sigh. 'But something did happen…?'

'Yes,' she confirmed huskily; what was the point in pretending otherwise? Rachel, she knew, despite being ill, was far too astute to be deceived by any prevarication she might make.

Rachel nodded, her gaze unwavering on Leonie's face. 'You know, don't you?' she murmured ruefully.

She swallowed hard, very aware of Luke standing a short distance away, unable to hear their conversation, but more than capable of asking her for an explanation for it once they were outside. 'I know,' she confirmed softly.

'And you would like to talk to me about it,' Rachel accepted gruffly.

'It can wait,' Leonie assured her, able to feel Luke's impatience rising as he stood glowering behind her in the doorway. Besides, even this brief conversation with Rachel was enough to tell Leonie that her worst suspicions were correct…!

'As it's already waited thirty-eight years, I suppose that it can,' Rachel acknowledged heavily. 'Come back and see me tomorrow, hmm? Without Luke,' she added unnecessarily.

'If Michael says I may.' Leonie nodded. 'There really is no hurry, Rachel.' She briefly squeezed the other woman's hand.

'I think there is,' Rachel murmured huskily, sudden tears swimming in those dark green eyes.

Leonie looked at her concernedly, a sudden heaviness in her own chest at the unspoken message she read in Rachel's expressive green eyes.

She drew her breath in sharply. 'I'll come back tomorrow,' she promised Rachel softly. 'Alone.'

'Good.' Rachel smiled, relaxing back on her pillows with obvious relief. 'And don't worry, Leonie; things are never quite as black—or white—as they appear to be.'

Leonie wasn't so sure about that as she silently limped out of the hospital room ahead of Luke. What she had read just now in Rachel's eyes—

'What did my mother say to you?' Luke predictably demanded to know once they were outside in the carpeted corridor.

Leonie thought quickly. 'She asked if I would telephone Janet and ask her to bring some of Rachel's things in for her,' she improvised abruptly. 'I think it was less embarrassing to ask me,' she added.

'I see,' Luke dismissed uninterestedly, obviously accepting the explanation. 'I think it's time I found Michael,' he muttered grimly.

'Of course.' Leonie nodded. 'I'm sure you would rather talk to him alone so I'll—'

'Stay with me, Leonie,' Luke rasped, his hand suddenly painful on her arm as he turned her to face him, his face darkly pleading.

She looked at him, could clearly see the strain he was under, deep lines grooved beside his eyes and mouth, that nerve once again pulsing in his clenched jaw. She swallowed hard, nodding wordlessly.

'Thank you.' Luke's arms moved about her as he held her against the warmth of his chest.

Leonie was aware of his heart beating erratically, of the slight tremor of his arms as he held her against him, easily recognising that beneath his outward anger he was desperately upset and worried about his mother.

If what Leonie had read in the other woman's eyes a few minutes ago was what she had thought it was, then she knew Luke had every right to be upset and worried...

CHAPTER TWELVE

'THIS is very kind of you.' Luke smiled at her grate-
fully as she placed the plate of omelette and salad in
front of him on her dining-table.

As she had known she was to be away for most of
the weekend Leonie hadn't bothered to get any fresh
food in; omelette and tomato salad was the best she
had been able to come up with after inviting Luke to
stop and have dinner with her at her apartment before
he went back to the clinic this evening to visit his
mother.

Although, as she sat down beside Luke with her own
meal, and watched him pick half-heartedly at the food,
she knew he was still too worried about Rachel to be
able to eat very much, anyway.

Leonie had insisted on waiting in the car while Luke
went to talk to Michael, and apart from a few muttered
comments when he'd rejoined her, such as, 'Michael
insists it was a mild attack, whatever that might be!'
she had no idea what conversation had taken place between the two men. But, remembering the look that
had passed between Rachel and herself earlier, Leonie
would hazard a guess that Michael still hadn't told
Luke everything...

'I'm sorry.' Luke gave a rueful grimace now. 'I'm
afraid I'm not very good company today.'

'No one is expecting you to be,' Leonie assured him.
'It's all been a bit of a shock for you.'

He sighed heavily, putting down his knife and fork

as he gave up any pretence of eating the meal she had prepared for him. 'I suppose everyone expects their parents to go on for ever—until something like this happens and you realise it just isn't so.'

It must be even worse for Luke; he had only ever had the one parent.

Until now...

Was that why—? Could that be the reason—? She really did have to talk to Rachel!

Leonie reached over and lightly touched Luke's hand. 'Rachel is a very strong personality; she'll bounce back from this, you'll see.' She smiled encouragingly, hoping that she was speaking the truth. About the mild heart attack, at least...

'I hope so.' Luke nodded, but he didn't look convinced. 'Look, I've been thinking about yesterday evening, Leonie, and—'

'Yesterday evening?' she echoed sharply.

'Hmm.' Luke gave a grimace. 'I've realised that perhaps I wasn't exactly—tactful, last night. I shouldn't have mentioned your adoption. I—'

'Oh, that!' Leonie said with some relief. 'Don't give it another thought, Luke.' She shook her head. 'It's just been a taboo subject in my family for so long—my mother was furious with me when I put it in my grandfather's biography!—I was surprised, that's all,' she dismissed.

She had thought for a moment that he was referring to something else about yesterday evening!

'But you've been upset ever since.' He shook his head. 'I had no right—'

'I've said it doesn't matter, Luke,' she told him firmly; this subdued, apologetic Luke was so unlike the man she was used to that she just wanted the other

Luke back. Although, with his mother ill in hospital, she realised it might be some time before that happened.

He turned his hand over, his fingers tightly gripping hers, his gaze intense on her face as he looked at her searchingly. 'Leonie—' He broke off as the doorbell rang.

Leonie frowned at the sound, couldn't imagine who her caller could be at six-thirty on a Sunday evening. But at the same time she was pleased at the interruption. There was still so much she didn't know—so much she was sure Luke didn't know!—that she didn't consider it a good idea for the two of them to become any closer than they already were.

'I'll just get that.' She released her hand as she stood up. 'It's probably someone trying to sell me something,' she added.

'On a Sunday evening?' Luke murmured doubtfully.

'An ideal time to find most people at home,' she pointed out ruefully, moving out of the room and down the hallway to her front door. 'Jeremy...?' She stared at him as she found him standing on her doorstep for the second time in as many days.

He grinned unabashedly. 'I was worried about you. Because of your ankle,' he explained as Leonie looked puzzled. 'So I thought I would come round and see how you were, and check if you need a lift into work in the morning?'

She hadn't given her ankle much thought in the last few hours—in view of Rachel's hospitalisation it seemed totally irrelevant. But what she was very aware of was Luke's presence only a few feet away in her sitting-room!

'You could have telephoned and asked me that,' she

answered without thinking, at once realising how un-
grateful she sounded. 'I'm sure I'm going to be able to
drive in the morning,' she added in what she hoped
was a less caustic tone.

'That's good.' Jeremy smiled. 'I must say, you seem
a lot better.'

'I am.' She nodded, wishing he would just go now
she had told him what he wanted to know. But instead
he just stood there looking at her. 'I was actually just
going to have a soak in the bath,' she added pointedly.

'That should help.' He nodded.

Any second now, Leonie knew, Luke was going to
come strolling out of her sitting-room, the two men
were going to confront each other, and—

Too late! Even as she guessed what was going to
happen next she heard a movement behind her, saw the
way Jeremy's eyes widened as his gaze moved past her
down the hallway. It had to be Luke...

'Everything okay, Leonie?' he drawled hardly as he
came to stand beside her, his gaze flinty with displeasure as he looked at the other man.

That was nothing to how Jeremy looked! Stunned
probably best described that.

Oh, well, there was only one thing for her to do now.
Well...two, actually, but turning tail and leaving the
two men to it really wasn't an option!

She stood to one side of the doorway so that the two
men could see each other better. 'Jeremy, this is Luke
Richmond,' she introduced lightly. 'Luke, Jeremy
Burnley.' She deliberately didn't give either man any
more information than that—mainly because she
wasn't sure what either of them were in her life any
more!

She supposed Jeremy could best be described as having been her boyfriend, but he wasn't any more—even if she hadn't told him that yet. Luke was the son of Rachel Richmond—but that wasn't all he was any more, either…!

The two men shook hands stiltedly, eyeing each other warily. Like two stags at bay, Leonie thought crossly.

'Well, if that was all, Jeremy—'

'Richmond,' he repeated slowly over the top of her dismissal. 'Rachel Richmond's son?' he prompted interestedly.

'And what if I am?' Luke bit out harshly.

'Nothing at all.' Once again Jeremy grinned unabashedly. 'It's okay, Leonie has told me all about the biography she's doing for your mother.'

Glacial silver-green eyes were suddenly turned on Leonie. 'Indeed?' Luke rasped coldly. Accusingly.

Leonie had given an inward groan of dismay at Jeremy's claim. Although, in reality, she couldn't exactly say it wasn't true. After all, he obviously did know about the biography, and in the circumstances it was obvious only she could have told him about it.

'Not all about it,' she corrected sharply, her gaze beseeching as she sought Luke's.

It was a plea that was met by glittering anger. Her heart sank at the realisation that he had taken Jeremy's words literally, that he now believed she had lied to him yesterday when she'd claimed Jeremy knew none of the details of his mother's biography.

She put out a hand. 'Luke—'

'If the two of you will excuse me—' Luke cut coldly across what was to have been her protest of innocence, totally ignoring her outstretched hand '—I have to get back to the hospital,' he bit out harshly.

Leonie let her hand fall back to her side, knowing there was no point in talking to him now, that with Jeremy here at the moment it would do no good, anyway.

'I'll talk to Janet about my mother's things, Leonie,' Luke rasped dismissively. 'Burnley,' he added scathingly as he passed the other man in the doorway, Leonie watching him as he took the steps back up to the pavement two at a time.

Leonie turned back to Jeremy, furiously angry. She might not have known earlier how to handle where her future with Luke was going—or if it were going anywhere!—but she certainly hadn't expected them to part under such bad terms!

'Thank you very much!' she snapped at Jeremy forcefully. 'You've now given Luke the impression that I go about discussing his mother's private business with every Tom, Dick or Harry!' Her cheeks were flushed with anger, eyes a glittering grey.

'Actually, it's Jeremy,' he said slowly, looking at her with puzzled eyes. 'Exactly what was he doing here anyway?' he prompted thoughtfully.

'He— I—' she broke off awkwardly, not quite knowing what to say next. 'His mother is ill in hospital,' she finally burst out.

'That's a shame,' Jeremy said mildly.

'Luke is naturally upset,' Leonie continued irritably.

'Naturally,' Jeremy acknowledged softly. 'That still doesn't explain what he was doing here, in your apartment,' he pointed out reasonably.

She drew in a sharp breath. 'Jeremy, we may be friends, but that doesn't give you the right to question other friendships in my life!' she snapped disgustedly, able to hear Luke's car now as he drove away.

Blond brows rose over guarded blue eyes. 'It doesn't...?'

'Of course it doesn't,' she dismissed impatiently. 'I don't ask you if you're meeting anyone else the evenings we don't see each other, do I?' She was breathing heavily in her agitation.

What must Luke think of her? She shook her head; yet another explanation that needed to be made. If Luke would let her make it, that was...

'I suppose not,' Jeremy conceded slowly. 'Leonie, am I to take it, from your remarks just now, that you and Richmond are actually involved?'

'No! I mean, yes! I don't know!' she cried, past caring now. Luke had left believing the worst of her, and she was in no mood to give Jeremy explanations for anything!

'You "don't know",' he repeated, mildly soft. 'I see.' His voice had hardened sharply now. 'Leonie, I was under the impression that our—what did you call it just now? Friendship, I believe? Yes, friendship,' he repeated the word with a derisive curl of his top lip. 'I thought our friendship meant something to you. To both of us,' he added pointedly.

'It did. It does,' she corrected. 'It's just that—'

'Richmond is a far better future prospect than an impoverished university lecturer,' Jeremy finished scathingly.

'How dare you?' Leonie gasped incredulously.

'How dare *I*?' he repeated scornfully. 'I'm not the one making a fool of myself! Don't you see, Leonie, with a man like Richmond there won't be any future? Once he's had what he wants from you he will just discard you—'

'Go, Jeremy,' she cut in sharply, her cheeks pale

now. 'Just go,' she repeated wearily. 'Before you say something—'

'That I'll regret? Or that you will?' he challenged, shaking his head disgustedly. 'Men like Luke Richmond only play with women like you, Leonie—'

'That is enough!' she bit out tautly. 'Jeremy, let's at least try and part as friends, hmm,' she encouraged huskily.

He looked at her coldly. 'I don't think so, thank you,' he scorned before turning sharply on his heel and leaving, also taking the steps two at a time.

But, unlike when Luke had departed so abruptly, Leonie felt nothing but relief as she heard the engine of Jeremy's car noisily departing.

She made her way wearily back into the sitting-room, the remains of the meal she and Luke had been sharing when Jeremy had arrived evidence of his abrupt departure.

Just from her apartment? Or from her life completely…?

'Leonie, have you seen the newspaper this morning?' her grandfather questioned tensely down the telephone line.

Leonie ran her hands through her tousled hair as she tried to wake up, sitting up in bed, having only managed to reach out from beneath the bedclothes to pick up the receiver of the ringing telephone a few seconds ago. For all the good it had done her; her grandfather's question made absolutely no sense to her whatsoever.

'What time is it?' She tried to focus on the bedside clock. 'Grandfather, it's only seven-thirty in the morning!' she protested incredulously.

'And some of us have been up for well over an hour

already,' he returned impatiently. 'And we've read our newspaper!' he added caustically.

'They don't deliver my newspaper here.' Leonie was very slowly coming awake. 'I usually pick one up on my way to work.' She wiped the sleep from her eyes, feeling as if her lids were weighed down with lead.

She had not had a good night's sleep—in fact, she was surprised she had slept at all!—and this early-morning telephone call from her grandfather was doing nothing for her already shattered nerves.

Her grandfather sighed. 'Leonie, why didn't you tell me you're writing Rachel Richmond's biography?'

'What?' She came fully awake now, her fingers tightly gripping the receiver. 'No one is supposed to know about that.' She frowned. 'How did you find out?'

'The same way everyone else who buys a newspaper today will find out—by reading it!' he told her tensely. 'Leonie, as you know, I take two newspapers: *The Times* for to-the-point news and the crossword, and a less reputable newspaper for the gossipy stuff.' He spoke more calmly now. 'Rachel's illness, and the fact that you're in the process of writing her biography, is on the front page of the latter,' he told her gently.

Leonie closed her eyes, falling back against her rumpled pillows, feeling nauseous. How on earth—?

Jeremy...!

There could be no other explanation; the amount of people who were aware of the work she was doing for Rachel could be counted on one hand—and none of those other people was likely to have leaked such a story to the press.

A fact Luke, when he was made aware of the article, would also no doubt be aware of...

Only Jeremy, Leonie knew, had been feeling vindictive enough when he'd left here last night to have done something like this. It wasn't going to take Luke long to work that out, either.

'Why didn't you tell me about the biography, Leonie?' her grandfather prompted again.

Leonie's brain was racing as she tried to think of ways to explain exactly what had happened to Luke when she next saw him. No matter which way she looked at it, it still came down to the fact that she was the one who had told Jeremy about the biography—and Rachel's illness, she now realised!—and as such she had to be held responsible for his having leaked that information to the press, too.

Luke was going to be furious—even more furious!—with her.

'Leonie?' her grandfather pushed impatiently.

She sighed. 'I didn't tell you because I was asked not to talk to anyone about it.' Something she seemed to have forgotten when she'd confided in Jeremy! 'Besides,' she added flatly, 'I had no idea you would be in the least interested.'

Her grandfather was quiet for several long seconds. 'But now you do?' he said quietly.

'I think so,' Leonie confirmed heavily, clearly remembering her grandfather's shock on Saturday evening at seeing Luke again. At the time she had just thought it had been because she hadn't arrived with Jeremy, now she wasn't so sure...

'I see,' he said slowly. 'At the party on Saturday evening, I expect?'

'Yes,' she acknowledged abruptly; what else could she say?

'I knew I should have pressed harder that evening concerning your friendship with Luke—'

'Not any more,' Leonie assured him ruefully. 'Luke is never going to forgive me for that newspaper article about his mother's illness and the biography,' she explained huskily.

'You didn't give them the story, did you?' Her grandfather sounded absolutely astounded.

'Of course not,' she dismissed impatiently. 'But I believe a friend of mine may have done,' she added heavily.

'A question of a man scorned, is that it?' he guessed accurately.

'Something like that.' She grimaced, sure it had to have been Jeremy. 'I really don't want to talk about this any more just now, Grandfather. I have to find Luke and try to explain—'

'I believe you and I need to talk too, Leonie,' he put in firmly.

'Not now, Grandfather,' she said pleadingly. If she couldn't find Luke, she could at least explain to Rachel what had happened. Besides, she and Rachel needed to talk anyway...

'It's waited all these years, it can wait a little longer, hmm?' he acknowledged dryly.

'Grandfather, I—' No, she couldn't tell him about Rachel!

What good would it do, after all these years? Besides, she wasn't sure yet whether her guess concerning the other woman's state of health was a correct one. Until she did, she would be better not saying anything to anyone else.

Now, when Jeremy had broken her confidence so blatantly, she had the foresight to realise that!

'I'll call you later on today, okay?' she prompted instead, sitting up to swing her legs out of bed.

Her ankle, she noted thankfully, was much less painful and swollen today. Swollen or not, it was going to have to stand up to her walking and driving with it, because she intended calling in sick today in order to go and see Rachel.

Her grandfather drew in a sharp breath. 'Try not to think too badly about this situation until the two of us have talked, hmm? Things are never quite what they seem, you know,' he added gently.

'It's Luke I'm most concerned about,' she told him honestly.

'Yes,' her grandfather accepted huskily. 'I have to say, what little I've seen of him, I think he's a rather remarkable young man.'

To Leonie, he was so much more than that!

But he had been angry enough with her last night for what he considered her betrayal of his mother—how much more angry was he going to be with her today after the appearance of that newspaper article...?

CHAPTER THIRTEEN

'YOU'VE guessed that I'm dying, haven't you, Leonie?' There was no bitterness or regret in Rachel's voice as she lay in the hospital bed smiling wistfully at Leonie—just a mere statement of fact.

Leonie, although she had suspected as much yesterday, was the one left reeling.

Rachel was *dying*?

No, it simply couldn't be true!

Leonie had tried calling Luke at Rachel's home before leaving her apartment this morning, but the ever-efficient Janet had told her that he wasn't there. Not that Leonie had thought he would have been, but she had no idea of the telephone number of his London apartment and, very much doubting that Janet, who hardly knew her, would give it to her, she hadn't bothered to ask her for it, either.

Rachel had been alone when Leonie had arrived shortly after ten o'clock, but she had seemed pleased to see her. She looked so much better today, the colour back in her cheeks, her full make-up in place, even her hair freshly washed and styled. Leonie simply couldn't believe that she was dying.

'It's true, I'm afraid,' Rachel said gently in answer to the involuntary shake Leonie had given of her head. 'Michael, dear man that he is, had the awful job of confirming it for me several months ago.'

'But you seem so much better today. Surely—'

'Oh, this little heart attack is nothing, Leonie,' the

165

other woman assured her. 'You see, I have an inoperable cancer,' she said softly. 'I would much rather I hadn't, of course.' She continued talking to give Leonie chance to get over her obvious shock. 'I did so want to see Luke married, perhaps bounce a grandchild or two on my knee,' she added wistfully. 'But it isn't to be, I'm afraid.'

Leonie blinked back the sudden tears. 'How—? When—?'

'A year, possibly, if I'm lucky,' Rachel answered the question Leonie was too distressed to be able to ask. 'Please don't be upset.' She reached out and took Leonie's hand in hers, smiling mishievously. 'I've had a simply marvellous life. I've done more or less what I wanted. I've had my career. Travelled. Brought up a wonderful son.' Her voice broke slightly as she spoke of Luke. 'He's my only regret, Leonie.' Tears flooded the deep green eyes. 'When I'm gone—'

'Please don't!' Leonie said brokenly, her hand tight on the other woman's.

'Leonie.' Rachel reached up to gently cup one side of Leonie's face with her hand. 'I'm seventy-five years old, have already had five years longer than my allotted three-score-and-ten; I've told you, my only regret is Luke.' She lay back with a sigh, seeming suddenly tired. 'Because of— Circumstances mean that he will be all alone once I'm gone. That I do regret.'

Leonie looked searchingly at the other woman, and what she saw in that beautiful troubled face brought her to a decision. 'But we both know that isn't true— don't we?' she said softly.

Rachel turned her head to look at Leonie, smiling ruefully. 'Do we?'

'His father—'

'When I talked to Luke last night he would tell me very little about the weekend the two of you spent in Devon with your family.' Rachel's eyes sparkled eagerly. 'Did the two of them meet? Talk to each other?' She looked suddenly anxious.

'They did,' Leonie confirmed lightly. 'This is the reason you chose me to write your biography, isn't it?' she said knowingly, having thought long and hard about all of this when she hadn't been able to sleep the previous night; she had come to some pretty incredible conclusions! 'Tell me, did you ever really intend to have the biography published?'

Rachel laughed softly, shaking her head. 'No,' she admitted huskily. 'I would never do a thing like that to Luke.'

Leonie had always known that. Which was why she had always been so puzzled concerning Rachel's determination to have her write her biography. But over the weekend, when she'd seen Luke and his father together, she had guessed at least some of the reason for Rachel's determination. Of course, she hadn't known then that Rachel wanted Luke to meet and get to know his father because she was dying...

She swallowed hard. 'Just how much of this does Luke know?'

Rachel shrugged. 'Well, he knows who his father is, of course—'

'He does?' Leonie gasped.

'I told him years ago.' Rachel nodded. 'Do you remember our telling you that he went off to starve in a garret for a couple of years?'

Leonie smiled. 'I remember—he didn't starve!'

'No, well, he wouldn't, would he?' Rachel acknowledged proudly. 'Luke is much too talented and self-sufficient to ever do that!' She sobered. 'No, when Luke was twenty-five he finally asked me who his father was. I told him, of course. I had decided years ago that I would if he ever asked. Well, he asked,' she sighed. 'Those two years he lived away from me were spent in search of who he really was.' She smiled emotionally, her eyes swimming with tears. 'He finally came back and told me that my son was who he really was, that the rest was unimportant.'

Leonie found she was also fighting back the tears. Poor Luke. And poor Rachel. But if Luke had known for twelve years who his father was…?

'But all of that's changed now…?' she prompted huskily, able to see all too clearly how Rachel, once she'd learned of her terminal illness, had reasoned things out in her mind. Luke didn't have to be left alone in the world when he had a father who was still living. Albeit the two men didn't know each other, but that didn't alter the fact that they were father and son.

Rachel sighed. 'Of course. Luke has a family, Leonie. Your family. I've asked for nothing for myself all these years, but when it comes to Luke…!' She shook her head. 'I would do anything for my son, Leonie.'

'I know that.' Leonie nodded. And she did, only too well. 'But are you sure Luke wants this particular family?' She frowned.

If Rachel had told Luke twelve years ago who his father was, then he had known on Saturday evening that he was in his presence. But not by word or action had he given the slightest inclination the other man was any more than a newly made acquaintance. Leonie had only guessed at the relationship herself because the resemblance between the two men was so obvious. To her, at least.

'He liked Leo when he met him last year.' Rachel frowned. 'He likes you too,' she added softly.

Leonie grimaced. 'Maybe he did…' She drew in a deep breath. 'Rachel, the newspapers today—'

'Oh, I've seen those,' the other woman dismissed uninterestedly.

'You have?' Leonie gasped; she had been dreading confessing to Rachel about those newspaper articles.

She had picked a newspaper up on her drive in to the clinic, stopping to have a coffee too so that she didn't arrive at too early an hour. Her grandfather was right, the newspaper articles were intrusively revealing.

Rachel smiled. 'Luke came in to see me at eight o'clock this morning. He had the newspapers with him. He was a little angry,' she admitted at Leonie's anxious expression.

A little? Leonie was sure he had been blazing! Like her, he had probably had little difficulty in guessing the newspaper's source, either…!

But at least she had been reprieved from facing him just yet—it had been her worst nightmare that he would actually be visiting with his mother when she arrived this morning.

She swallowed hard. 'I'm sure he was.' She grimaced again. 'That's what I mean, Rachel. Luke may like my grandfather, and there's no doubting that he was comfortable with the family on Saturday evening, but he's sure to hold me responsible for those newspaper articles, and—'

'Not in the least,' Rachel cut in firmly. 'He seemed in no doubt as to where the blame for that lay.' She gave Leonie a pointed look.

As she had thought, Luke had guessed it was Jeremy… 'Er—where is Luke this morning?' she asked warily.

Rachel shook her head. 'He didn't say where he was going, only that he will be back later this evening.'

Leonie frowned worriedly, very much afraid that she knew exactly where Luke had gone…!

Rachel reached out and squeezed her hand reassuringly. 'Please don't worry about it, Leonie; I very much doubt that Luke will do any lasting damage to your young man.'

'He isn't my young man any longer,' Leonie assured her with feeling. And it wasn't Jeremy she was worried about! Not that she didn't think Luke was more than capable of taking care of himself, she just didn't think it a good idea for him to come in here to see his mother looking as if he had been in a bar-room brawl.

'That's probably just as well.' Rachel patted her hand. 'My mother told me something quite interesting about men when I was still in my teens,' she continued musingly. 'She said that tall men are invariably amiable and easygoing, because they have nothing to prove, but short men tend to turn spiteful if they feel in the least inadequate or threatened—which they very often do. It's a golden rule that has proved most helpful over the years,' she added dismissively.

Leonie could only stare at the other woman. Luke had actually discussed Jeremy with his mother…? He had to have done for Rachel to mention Jeremy's height.

'Actually, I don't think Jeremy considers himself short at five feet ten inches tall,' she said dryly, still wrestling with the problem as to why Luke should have told his mother even that much about Jeremy.

'But, at six feet four inches tall, Luke obviously does!' His mother laughed indulgently. 'Just think, Leonie,' she added teasingly. 'You won't have to wear flat-heeled shoes now you aren't going out with him any more!'

Leonie returned her smile. 'I fell over my own feet the last time I wore heeled shoes!'

'You'll soon adjust,' Rachel assured her with certainty. 'It just takes a little practice. You—'

'Rachel...?'

Leonie froze as that familiar voice spoke with quivering uncertainty behind her, both women turning towards the door, Rachel frowning her puzzlement as she looked at the tall man who stood in the open doorway.

Leonie felt no such puzzlement as she looked at him, drawing in a shaky breath as she slowly stood up, at the same time giving him what she hoped was a reassuring smile. She had no idea what he was doing here, or even how he came to be here, but she suddenly felt very much as if she shouldn't be here to witness this...

She watched as the colour came and then went in Rachel's cheeks as she stared at the man. 'Tom...?' she finally breathed uncertainly.

Leonie's favourite uncle. Her great-uncle Tom. The brother-in-law of her grandfather.

But most importantly he was Luke's father...!

Could that possibly be the reason Uncle Tom had always subconsciously been her favourite uncle...? Or could it be the other way round; she had fallen in love with Luke because she had sensed that connection between him and her favourite relative? Leonie really had no answer to that puzzle, she only knew that she loved Luke. And that, no matter what Rachel might say to the contrary, he probably hated her for the appearance of those articles in the newspapers this morning.

She also still had no idea how two such different people as Rachel and Tom had ever met, let alone become involved with each other, but she had realised on Saturday evening, as she'd looked across the room as Tom and Luke had talked together, that they had to be father and son.

They were both tall, dark-haired, had those same patrician features, their smiles so achingly similar.

Tom's throat moved convulsively as he stared at the woman in the bed. 'The same can't be said of me, I'm afraid—but you haven't changed a bit, Rachel!' he said wonderingly.

'It is you, Tom…!' Tears glistened in dark green eyes as Rachel held her hand out to him invitingly.

'I'll—er—leave you two to talk,' Leonie said awkwardly, having the answer to how Uncle Tom happened to be here as she spotted her grandfather hovering outside in the corridor; he must have driven up from Devon directly after talking to her earlier this morning.

Perhaps it was just as well, Leonie reasoned as she moved towards the door, completely unnoticed by Tom and Rachel, who seemed to have eyes for no one but each other. It was time—past time!—that this muddle was resolved. One way or another.

It was not the time, however, for Luke to come striding purposefully down the corridor, his gaze narrowing suspiciously as he saw Leonie and her grandfather standing outside his mother's room.

Goodness knew what he was going to say when he discovered Tom—his father—was actually inside the room talking to Rachel!

CHAPTER FOURTEEN

'LUKE!' Leonie's grandfather greeted cheerfully even as he carefully closed the door to Rachel's room, moving deliberately down the corridor to meet the younger man, obviously having seen the direction of Leonie's horrified gaze—and decided to act upon it.

'Leo,' Luke returned slowly, shaking the other man's proffered hand, his gaze moving past the older man to rest on Leonie as she stood down the hallway looking defensive. 'Leonie,' he added tersely.

He didn't look as if he had been involved in a barroom brawl, after all, she decided with some relief, not a blemish to be seen on his handsome features, even if his expression was rather grim.

'Luke,' she greeted brightly, moving to join the two men, linking her arm companionably with her grandfather's as she looked up at Luke. 'I was just suggesting to Grandfather that we go for a coffee; perhaps you would like to join us?'

Luke still frowned. 'I need to see my mother—'

'She's resting,' Leonie put in quickly, aware that Rachel and Tom needed privacy for their conversation—even from their son! 'Too many visitors already this morning, I think,' she added firmly as Luke looked about to argue the point.

His gaze was glacial on hers. 'And whose fault is that, do you think?' he rasped pointedly.

The colour warmed her cheeks. 'I have apologised

173

and explained the situation to Rachel,' she said resentfully.

Luke's mouth twisted humourlessly. 'And I have "explained" to Burnley that if he ever does anything like that again he will have more than just me to answer to!'

Leonie couldn't meet his gaze now. 'He won't,' she assured huskily.

'How about that coffee?' Her grandfather cut cheerfully through the awkward silence that followed this statement.

'Perhaps I should just go in and tell Rachel—'

'No!'

'No!'

'She's sleeping,' Leonie said more calmly, as both she and her grandfather had protested loudly at Luke's suggestion.

Green eyes narrowed as Luke looked from Leonie to her grandfather, and then back again. 'Who's in there with her?' he murmured shrewdly.

Leonie should have realised that Luke wouldn't be fooled for a moment by their jumpy behaviour; he was far too astute for that.

'Who do you think is in there, Luke?' her grandfather was the one to prompt gently.

He stared at the older man for long, unfathomable minutes.

So long, it seemed to Leonie she would never breathe again! What was Luke going to do when he realised his father was in there talking to his mother? Would he burst in, demanding that Tom leave? Or would he simply join them, and listen to what they had to say to each other? At this particular moment, remembering the expressions on Rachel's and Tom's faces as they'd looked at each other, Leonie didn't feel either of those courses of action was applicable.

Luke straightened, shrugging slightly. 'Where were you thinking of going for coffee?' he said mildly.

Leonie stared at him. She could have sworn—

'Close your mouth, Leonie,' he added derisively, smiling slightly. 'I'm not completely insensitive, you know.'

She hadn't realised her mouth was open until Luke had drawn attention to it, closing it with a decisive snap. 'I never thought you were,' she bit out irritably.

'No?' He raised mocking brows.

'No!' she snapped, glaring at him now.

'I noticed a lounge as we came in where they seemed to be serving coffee and tea,' her grandfather put in with amusement. 'I have a feeling that it isn't only Rachel and Tom that need to have a little talk,' he added pointedly.

Leonie shot Luke a resentful glance as they all walked down the hallway to the lounge where they were serving coffee. Her grandfather was wrong, she had nothing whatsoever to say to Luke when he was in this derisive mood.

'What exactly did you do to Jeremy?' she asked as soon as they had all sat down in the otherwise deserted lounge together, a pot of coffee and three cups having been requested from the receptionist outside.

Luke's eyes were glacial. 'Frightened I might have marred those boyish good looks of his?' he taunted.

Leonie drew in an angry breath. 'No—'

'Luke, this sort of conversation is entirely unproductive,' her grandfather cut in mildly.

'Maybe.' The younger man bared his teeth in what

was meant to pass as a smile. 'But it makes me feel a whole lot better!'

Her grandfather raised silver brows. 'For how long?'

Luke grimaced. 'Good point,' he murmured, turning to Leonie. 'I apologise for that last remark.' He gave an abrupt inclination of his head. 'I understand from Burnley that the two of you are no longer—friends?'

She swallowed hard. 'Why do you think he went to the newspapers with that story about your mother?' She shrugged dismissively.

Luke shrugged. 'Rachel has a theory about that—'

'She told me,' Leonie cut in ruefully.

'Did she?' He smiled. 'Why do *you* think Burnley did what he did?'

'Jealousy,' she answered instantly—and just as instantly regretted it. There was only one person in her life that Jeremy could possibly feel jealous about!

'Perhaps I should leave the two of you alone to talk…' her grandfather put in softly.

'No!' Leonie protested alone this time, turning uncertainly to look at Luke as he said nothing. 'No…?' she repeated slowly.

'I think, Leo—' Luke might have been speaking to her grandfather, but the force of his gaze didn't leave Leonie '—that there will be another time for Leonie and I to talk—at the moment she's probably more in need of a few explanations concerning what is going on back there.' He nodded in the direction of his mother's room.

She moistened dry lips, choosing her words carefully. 'I already know that Tom is your father.'

Luke nodded. 'But are you also aware that he doesn't know that?'

'He does now,' Leonie's grandfather put in softly,

giving a rueful shrug as Leonie and Luke turned to look at him. 'I thought, after Saturday evening, that it was only fair to tell him the truth, and so I rang him this morning after I had seen the report of Rachel's illness in the newspaper. Tom and I had a long and frank discussion before I drove him here. I still believe I did the right thing,' he added firmly as Leonie and Luke continued to look at him.

Leonie was still stunned by the fact that all these years Tom hadn't even known he had a son. Although it did explain so many things that had been puzzling her. Such as why Tom, a man she had always loved and looked up to, had seemingly abandoned Rachel to the fate of single-motherhood all these years. Such as why, when Leonie had been able to realise his relationship to Luke on Saturday evening, Tom himself had given no indication that he'd recognised Luke as his son.

Incredible as it seemed, he simply hadn't known he had a son!

'But how—? Why—?' She broke off, shaking her head, desperately trying to make sense of what her grandfather was saying. 'I don't understand,' she finally admitted with a frown.

'Tom was married when I was conceived, Leonie,' Luke began.

'To my sister Sally,' her grandfather continued, sighing heavily. 'Sally was driving herself up to London when she was involved in an accident. She was in hospital for months, had injured her spine, but it wasn't until almost a year later, all the options exhausted, that the doctors finally told her she would never walk again. I—she was my sister, and I loved her dearly, but after that she changed, became—hard, detached, especially to Tom. Of all things, I was working as the historical advisor of the film *Beloved Tsarina* at the time—'

'That wasn't in the biography,' Leonie said dazedly.

'No,' her grandfather acknowledged ruefully. 'I thought, taking into account the timing of it all, that the less people who knew about that connection, the better. Tom came to see me there on the set one day, out of his head with despair at the deterioration of his relationship with Sally; his marriage was in tatters, and he simply didn't know what to do. That was the day he and Rachel met each other,' he concluded simply. 'I believe it was love at first sight.'

Leonie understood that much. At least, as far as it went…

Her grandfather sighed. 'They tried to fight the attraction, of course,' he said firmly. 'Neither of them is the type of person to ever deliberately hurt someone else. But—they tried for months, but—well, the attraction proved too much, for both of them.' He shrugged. 'I knew of the relationship, of course; I would have been blind not to have done. But I also knew how much Tom had tried to help Sally, how he had stuck by her despite the fact that most of the time she seemed to hate him.' He shook his head. 'I'm not sure what happened, whether Sally guessed or even heard of the affair, or if she really did come to terms with her disability, but, three months into Tom's relationship with Rachel, Sally told him that she realised how awful she had been to him, that she—she wanted to make their marriage work. She asked him for a second chance.'

'And Tom, being the honourable man I believe him to be, despite being in love with another woman, knew that he had to give his wife that chance,' Luke put in huskily.

'Yes,' Leo acknowledged gruffly. 'There was no way, even loving Rachel as he did, that he could tell Sally, a woman who had already lost so much, that their marriage was over. So he agreed to a reconciliation. It was an agreement he made completely ignorant of Rachel's pregnancy,' he added softly.

Luke nodded. 'She told me that she didn't think it fair to Tom to put any more emotional pressure on him—'

'But she was expecting his child!' Leonie cried emotionally. 'She was expecting you,' she reminded Luke brokenly.

'Yes,' he acknowledged gently. 'But do you think either of them would have had a moment's happiness together knowing they had taken it at the cost of a woman who was already suffering enough? A woman who would never walk again, let alone be able to have the child Rachel knew she was going to have? And what good would it have done Tom to know that Rachel Richmond's love-child was in fact his child too?' Luke reasoned huskily as he seemed to anticipate Leonie's next question. 'It would have made his life with Sally a living hell.' He shook his head.

Leonie thought back over the years, to the numerous family occasions when Tom and Sally had both been present. She had no idea how the two had fared in those early years of Sally's disability, but in the latter years, even if they hadn't appeared to be madly in love with each other, the two had certainly been the best of friends. Perhaps it wasn't everyone's idea of a perfect marriage, but Tom and Sally had seemed to come to some sort of caring understanding of the limitations of their marriage.

Leonie shook her head. 'But when Rachel had her baby did it never even occur to Tom…?'

'I don't think Tom was in any shape at that time to even think about it.' Once again it was her grandfather who answered her. 'When he and Rachel decided to end their relationship, they agreed it had to be a complete break, with no contact whatsoever between them. Tom looked like hell for the next year or so,' Leo recalled gruffly. 'I'm not even sure he was aware Rachel had even had a baby.'

'But you were,' Leonie realised slowly.

He gave a shaky sigh. 'Rachel made me promise not to tell him. It was a promise I kept until this morning.'

'But now he knows.' Once again Luke glanced down the corridor towards his mother's room. 'How did he take it?'

Was it only Leonie's imagination, or was there a trace of anxiety in his voice…?

Her grandfather smiled warmly. 'The way any man would take being told you were his son! Initially he was stunned. But once the idea had taken hold, I could see the pride just bursting out of him.' He reached over to briefly clasp Luke's arm. 'He's a good man, Luke. One of the best,' he added emotionally.

'I've always known that if my mother loved him then he had to be,' Luke confirmed gruffly. 'Do you think he and Rachel…?' Once again he looked anxious.

Leo shrugged. 'Who knows, Luke? It's been almost forty years. They're different people now. But stranger things have happened. Would you mind?'

Luke winced. 'There's more to this than how I would feel about it, I'm afraid.' He grimaced.

Leonie looked at him searchingly, noting his pallor,

the lines beside his eyes and mouth, the heavy frown between his eyes. 'Luke…?' She sat forward anxiously.

He turned to give her a strained smile. 'She's dying, Leonie,' he told her emotionally. 'I made Michael tell me the truth last night—Rachel is dying!' He buried his face in his hands as his iron control finally broke.

Leonie didn't hesitate, moving down onto the carpeted floor beside him, barely aware of her grandfather as he stood up to usher the woman who had finally arrived with the coffee tray out of the room before him, the door closing softly behind them.

'I know, Luke! I know…!' Leonie murmured brokenly, moving up to take him into her arms, cradling his head on her shoulder as she felt his pain as well as her own.

Luke's arms moved about her as he held her fiercely against him. 'I love you, Leonie,' he muttered into the damp warmth of her throat. 'I tried so hard not to, but—I love you!'

Leonie was overwhelmed by the admission, knew she owed him nothing less than the truth in return. 'I love you, too, Luke,' she told him with feeling.

He raised his head to look down at her, eyes still damp with tears. 'Even though I gave you every reason not to?' he murmured self-derisively.

She gave a shaky smile. 'I must admit, you haven't made it easy for me.'

His arms tightened about her. 'I had guessed what Rachel was up to with the biography, knew it was another attempt on her part to gently introduce me to my rightful family. She had tried once already, you see, when she persuaded me to visit Leo concerning writing the screenplay of his war years.' He shook his head. 'Once I realised who he was, I backed off completely.

Believe it or not, I was trying to be protective of your family these last few weeks by attempting to frighten you off writing the biography.'

Leonie did believe him. Now that she knew the truth, knew the circumstances of his birth, of Rachel's terminal illness, she could see exactly what Rachel had been trying to do these last months. She could also see how Luke, ignorant of Rachel's illness, would fight against such a move on his mother's part, to the point where he would be totally obnoxious to anyone else involved. Namely her!

'I even removed some rather damning photographs of Tom from my mother's albums before handing them over to you,' Luke admitted ruefully. 'Not exactly playing fair, but I didn't know what else to do.' He grimaced.

Leonie gave a rueful smile. 'But I fell in love with you anyway,' she admitted self-derisively.

'I have to admit, when a reporter friend of mine told me who the source had been for that article in the newspapers today, I began to have my hopes,' Luke said huskily. 'A visit to Burnley this morning at least confirmed for me that you had shown him the door after I left last night!'

Leonie frowned. 'I was so angry with him. He guessed how I felt about you, and he said—he said— Well, never mind what he said,' she dismissed impatiently; remembering Jeremy's insulting words was still enough to make her angry. 'Sufficient to say I was glad to be rid of him!'

Luke reached down and lifted her up to sit on his knees as he relaxed back in the chair with her held in his arms. '"Sticks and stones", my love. I've been hearing things said about me and my illegitimacy most of my life,' he murmured sadly. 'Besides, I had a few cutting things to say to you myself when I believed you were in love with Burnley!'

Leonie looked at him shyly. 'I had wondered myself if you might not be a little in love with Janet…?'

'Janet!' he repeated incredulously. 'Janet is in love with an out-of-work actor named Julian! And I am most certainly not in love with her. How could I be, when I'm in love with you?'

Leonie glowed in the warmth of that love. 'And now that you know I love you, too?'

He grinned. 'Now I know that I intend to show you only the kind, caring side of my nature. With only the occasional jealous lapse, probably,' he admitted ruefully.

'I think I can cope with that!' Leonie snuggled down in his arms, hardly able to believe that a day that had started out so badly had now become the happiest in her life. Luke loved her as much as she loved him!

'So what happens next, do you think?' Luke murmured into her hair.

'Well… Your mother mentioned earlier that she would like a grandchild. Or two,' she added huskily.

And then wished she hadn't as she felt Luke become very still, not even his chest moving as he even seemed to have stopped breathing.

What a fool she had been to assume— Okay, so Luke had said he loved her, but he hadn't said anything else, had he? Certainly not that he wanted to— In fact, he had once said the opposite!

'I'm sorry,' she choked, shaking her head. 'I remember now that you once said you would never marry and have children.'

His arms tightened about her. 'Until today I felt that

it wouldn't be fair for me to marry any woman. She would want to know about my father, and out of loyalty to my mother I would never be able to tell her. It would have put a strain on any marriage before it began.'

Leonie was very still. 'But that doesn't apply now...'

'No.' He drew a deep breath into his lungs. 'I'm afraid I have very old-fashioned ideas about having children, believe they should be brought up within a loving marriage.'

Leonie swallowed hard. 'Yes,' she finally managed to murmur.

His arms tightened about her painfully. 'Yes, you agree with me? Or yes, you will marry me?'

She moistened dry lips, keeping her head down on his chest. 'Yes, I agree with you. And... You haven't asked me yet!' There was no way she could answer his second question, not when his love was so new to her, and she had no way of knowing what he wanted from her!

He drew in a sharp breath. 'I'm not very good on rejection,' he admitted huskily.

Leonie briefly closed her eyes, knowing, because of her own adoption, how that felt. Perhaps this was a chance for both of them to make their own family, to belong to each other as they had belonged to no one else.

But for that to happen she had to look at him, had to let him see the love she felt for him. A love, she was sure, that would stand the test of time.

She raised her head, looking straight into the green depths of his eyes, instantly able to see her own love reflected back at her.

She shook her head. 'I'm not going to reject you,

Luke,' she assured him forcefully. 'I will never do that!' she added fiercely.

His hands moved to cup either side of her face as he stared at her intently. 'Will you marry me, Leonora Winston?'

'I will, Luke Richmond,' Leonie answered unhesitantly, smiling as she remembered when he had last called her by her full name, clearly remembering the antagonism between them on that initial meeting. How their emotions had changed in such a short time!

He gave a relieved groan as he held her fiercely to him. 'I don't know how Tom ever let my mother go if he loved her the way I love you!'

Leonie remembered the expression on Tom's face a short time ago as he'd looked across the room at Rachel. 'I'm not sure that he ever did…' she said emotionally. 'Would you mind if they were to—find each other again, after all this time?'

'Not in the least; I would be overjoyed for them.' Luke held her away from him, his gaze compelling. 'I'll never let you go, Leonie. Never!'

'I won't ever want you to,' she answered with certainty, before drawing in a deep breath. 'About Rachel—'

Luke put silencing gentle fingers on her lips. 'We will all continue to love and appreciate her for as much time as we have left with her,' Luke cut in firmly.

'Yes,' Leonie agreed determinedly.

As it happened, they had eighteen more wonderful months with Rachel before she left them.

Eighteen months, when the love she had always kept locked away in her heart for Tom was allowed to blossom once more, as his was for her, the two of them marrying at long last, making those last eighteen months the happiest Rachel—and Tom—had ever known.

Eighteen months, when Rachel did indeed hold her treasured grandchild on her knee. A little girl Leonie and Luke named Rachel, after her beloved grandmother...

Modern Romance™
...seduction and
passion guaranteed

Tender Romance™
...love affairs that
last a lifetime

Sensual Romance™
...sassy, sexy and
seductive

Blaze Romance™
...the temperature's
rising

Medical Romance™
...medical drama on
the pulse

Historical Romance™
...rich, vivid and
passionate

27 new titles every month.

*With all kinds of Romance for
every kind of mood...*

MILLS & BOON®

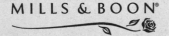

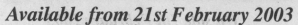

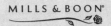

FREE!

2 Books
and a surprise gift!

We would like to take this opportunity to thank you for reading this Mills & Boon® book by offering you the chance to take TWO more specially selected titles from the Modern Rómance™ series absolutely FREE! We're also making this offer to introduce you to the benefits of the Reader Service™—

- ★ FREE home delivery
- ★ FREE gifts and competitions
- ★ FREE monthly Newsletter
- ★ Books available before they're in the shops
- ★ Exclusive Reader Service discount

Accepting these FREE books and gift places you under no obligation to buy; you may cancel at any time, even after receiving your free shipment. Simply complete your details below and return the entire page to the address below. *You don't even need a stamp!*

YES! Please send me 2 free Modern Romance books and a surprise gift. I understand that unless you hear from me, I will receive 4 superb new titles every month for just £2.55 each, postage and packing free. I am under no obligation to purchase any books and may cancel my subscription at any time. The free books and gift will be mine to keep in any case.

P3ZEB

Ms/Mrs/Miss/Mr ....Initials................................

BLOCK CAPITALS PLEASE

Surname...

Address...

....

....Postcode ....

Send this whole page to:
UK: The Reader Service, FREEPOST CN81, Croydon, CR9 3WZ
EIRE: The Reader Service, PO Box 4546, Kilcock, County Kildare (stamp required)